"Wel

Richard said.

"Wait." C.J. met his gaze, was instantly swept up in the power, the intensity, the heat. It was all she could do to keep herself from touching his freshly shaved chin, from pressing her palm against his face and whispering that there was nothing on earth she wanted more than to spend every evening of her life with him, and only with him.

She forced her thoughts away from that desire. "Umm. Would you like to take some cookies home for your daughter?"

"No, she's allergic to chocolate."

"That makes two of us," C.J. murmured as Richard helped himself to a cookie and took a slow, melting bite.

"Too bad," he said. "It's the food of the gods."

"Yes." It came out on a sigh. She reached out to wipe a crumb from his lips. "Better than sex."

Her eyes widened in horror. Had she actually said that out loud?

She had.

Dear Reader,

July brings you the fifth title of Silhouette Romance's VIRGIN BRIDES promotion. This series is devoted to the beautiful metaphor of the traditional white wedding and the fairy-tale magic of innocence awakened to passionate love on the wedding night. In perennial favorite Sandra Steffen's offering, *The Bounty Hunter's Bride,* a rugged loner finds himself propositioned by the innocent beauty who'd nursed him to health in a remote mountain cabin. He resists her precious gift…but winds up her shotgun groom when her father and four brothers discover their hideaway!

Diana Whitney returns to the Romance lineup with *One Man's Promise,* a wonderfully warmhearted story about a struggling FABULOUS FATHER and an adventurous single gal who are brought together by their love for his little girl and a shaggy mutt named Rags. And THE BRUBAKER BRIDES are back! In *Cinderella's Secret Baby,* the third book of Carolyn Zane's charming series, tycoon Mac Brubaker tracks down the poor but proud bride who'd left him the day after their whirlwind wedding, only to discover she's about to give birth to the newest Brubaker heir.…

Wanted: A Family Forever is confirmed bachelor Zach Robinson's secret wish in this intensely emotional story by Anne Peters. But will marriage-jaded Monica Griffith and her little girl trust him with their hearts? Linda Varner's twentieth book for Silhouette is book two of THREE WEDDINGS AND A FAMILY. When two go-getters learn they must marry to achieve their dreams, a wedding of convenience results in a *Make-Believe Husband*…and many sleepless nights! Finally, a loyal assistant agrees to be her boss's *Nine-to-Five Bride* in Robin Wells's sparkling new story, but of course this wife wants her new husband to be a *permanent* acquisition!

Enjoy each and every Silhouette Romance!

Regards,

Joan Marlow Golan

Joan Marlow Golan
Senior Editor Silhouette Books

Please address questions and book requests to:
Silhouette Reader Service
U.S.: 3010 Walden Ave., P.O. Box 1325, Buffalo, NY 14269
Canadian: P.O. Box 609, Fort Erie, Ont. L2A 5X3

ONE MAN'S PROMISE

Diana Whitney

Silhouette

R O M A N C E™

Published by Silhouette Books

America's Publisher of Contemporary Romance

If you purchased this book without a cover you should be aware
that this book is stolen property. It was reported as "unsold and
destroyed" to the publisher, and neither the author nor the
publisher has received any payment for this "stripped book."

To Rae Lovald, a doggy-mom extraordinaire, who has
been so very generous with her kindness and support.
Thanks a bunch, hon. Your friendship means so much.

SILHOUETTE BOOKS

ISBN 0-373-19307-6

ONE MAN'S PROMISE

Copyright © 1998 by Diana Hinz

All rights reserved. Except for use in any review, the reproduction
or utilization of this work in whole or in part in any form by any
electronic, mechanical or other means, now known or hereafter
invented, including xerography, photocopying and recording, or in
any information storage or retrieval system, is forbidden without
the written permission of the editorial office, Silhouette Books,
300 East 42nd Street, New York, NY 10017 U.S.A.

All characters in this book have no existence outside the imagination of
the author and have no relation whatsoever to anyone bearing the same
name or names. They are not even distantly inspired by any individual
known or unknown to the author, and all incidents are pure invention.

This edition published by arrangement with Harlequin Books S.A.

® and TM are trademarks of Harlequin Books S.A., used under license.
Trademarks indicated with ® are registered in the United States Patent
and Trademark Office, the Canadian Trade Marks Office and in other
countries.

Printed in U.S.A.

DIANA WHITNEY

says she loves "fat babies and warm puppies, mountain streams and California sunshine, camping, hiking and gold prospecting. Not to mention strong romantic heroes!" She married her own real-life hero twenty years ago. With his encouragement, she left her longtime career as a municipal finance director and pursued the dream that had haunted her since childhood—writing. To Diana, writing is a joy, the ultimate satisfaction. Reading, too, is her passion, from spine-chilling thrillers to sweeping sagas, but nothing can compare to the magic and wonder of romance. She loves to hear from readers. Write to her c/o Silhouette Books, 300 East 42nd Street, 6th floor, New York, NY 10017.

Hi, folks!

No one ever said being a father was easy. I knew it would be tough. I just didn't how *how* tough. Of course, my daughter, Lissa, can be a bit difficult at times. Not that I blame her. I mean, so what if she gets a little cranky now and again? It's not her fault that she's not like other kids. Lissa has always been fragile. Growing up motherless hasn't been easy for her, and I suppose I haven't been quite as strict as I should have been. It's hard to discipline a child who's been through so much in her young life. I've been worried about her.

But that was before C. J. Moray swirled into our lives with a dazzling smile and a zest for living that just naturally makes a person laugh out loud. C.J. has a way about her, a way of wriggling into a man's heart before he even knows what hit him.

As for Lissa, well, it seems I don't understand my daughter as well as I thought. But C.J. understands her all too well.

Oops, I've got to go. That nutty dog just crashed his skateboard again.

Sincerely,

Richard Matthews

Chapter One

Dear God, it *was* him. That hair, those eyes, the cocky strut. It had been so long, so achingly long.

C. J. Moray stomped the brake pedal, twisted the wheel to squeal a sloppy U-turn on the quiet residential street. Rubber burned, tires spun, screeched and hit the curb with a bounce, startling the daylights out of a jogger huffing up the sidewalk.

Jamming the car into Park, she leapt out with her heart in her throat, eyes focused on the one who had been such a huge part of her life for so very, very long.

He hadn't changed, was just as she remembered. So handsome, so regal, so deliciously wicked.

A young girl was talking to him, smiling, laughing, hugging him with the same affection C.J. herself had once lavished on him. As always, he reveled in the attention, dark eyes intensely focused, riveted on his giggling companion without sparing so much as a glance at the winded jogger.

The panting man bent over, propped his hands on his knees, gaping in astonishment as C.J. joyously rushed forward with open arms to call her beloved's name.

Perky ears twitched, a furry head swiveled, dark eyes blinked bright and gleaming.

"Rags! Come here, boy, c'mon!"

With a gleeful yelp, thirty pounds of quivering canine excitement sprinted down the sidewalk and bounded into her waiting arms.

Laughing and crying at the same time, C.J. hugged the warm, wriggling body of the animal she had raised from a pup and adored beyond measure. "Oh, Rags—" She sputtered under a frantic assault of wet doggy kisses. "Wait...stop...silly boy!"

When the affectionate assault eased, she felt the lump rise back in her throat, softening her voice to a smoky whisper. "I thought I'd never see you again."

Rags barked in her face, licked off her eye makeup. C.J. felt as if her heart would explode from sheer happiness.

Then their joyful reunion was interrupted by a distressed wail. "Da-addy!" The abandoned girl stamped her feet. "That lady is stealing my dog! Make her stop, Daddy, make her stop!"

Rags responded by leaping down and dashing back to comfort the tearful youngster, who clamped a proprietary hand on the animal's collar and fixed C.J. with an eat-dirt-and-die look.

C.J.'s lungs deflated like a pricked balloon. She forced a smile, and since the child was kneeling beside her bright-eyed pet, she squatted down to their level. "My name is C.J. Actually it's Cecelia Jane, but that's quite a mouthful, so my friends call me C.J.'' The child continued to glare silently. C.J. sucked a breath, tried to keep her smile from flattening. "So, now you know my name. Perhaps you'd like to tell me yours?"

The girl, a brown-haired, pigtailed nymph who appeared to be nine or ten, narrowed her eyes, clamped her lips together and continued to glower at C.J. as if wishing her dead.

"Her name is Lissa Matthews, and she's not usually so rude." The jogger, having recovered his breath, stepped forward, waited until C.J. stood before extending his hand. "I apologize for my daughter's lack of courtesy, Ms.—?"

"Moray." His grip was warm, firm. Damp tendrils of dark hair the same shade as his daughter's clung to a face attractively average, yet more appealing than most. She smiled through her scrutiny. "Please call me C.J."

A pleasant light gleamed in eyes that were neither gray nor green, but a hazy combination that reminded her of heather sage. "Richard Matthews. Please call me Richard." His hand lingered, withdrew slowly. "Well." Clearing his throat, he shifted uncomfortably, rubbed his knuckles across a strong, slightly clefted chin. "May I assume you and my daughter's pet share more than a passing acquaintance?"

C.J. confirmed that with a nod. "Rags and I were together for nearly six years." Stupidly, tears stung her eyes at the sight of her shaggy-faced best friend firmly ensconced in the arms of another. "He disappeared a couple of months ago, while my roommate was moving our things to a new apartment."

Richard Matthews didn't seem unsympathetic, but was

clearly concerned about the effect C.J.'s sudden appearance was having upon his daughter. His eyes narrowed just a touch, an expression of contemplation, or perhaps puzzlement. "We adopted the animal from the shelter. It's quite legal." Skimming a worried glance at the tearful child, he clasped his hands behind his back, facing C.J. with stiffened resolve. "Except for the collar engraved with his name, the animal had no identifying tags."

"I know—"

"Nor was there a proper dog license from which the owners could be located." The man tightened his jaw, angled a reproachful glance. "Not the behavior of a responsible pet owner, I'd say."

"You're right, of course, it's just that—" C.J. licked her lips, nervously flexed her fingers. "Both tags were on a collar ring. My roommate had removed it to replace the old address tag with the new one when the movers broke a vase or something, and Rags bolted out the front door. She put up flyers all over the neighborhood—"

"And you were where when all this happened?"

"I was, er, unavailable." She slipped a glance at the prancing pup, and her heart melted. God, she'd missed him so much. "I still have the tags. I can show them to you, if you wish."

Richard's chin wobbled. "That won't be necessary. I believe you. Still, this is a most unfortunate situation." He heaved a sigh, rubbed his face, peered over his fingertips. "Clearly, we have a legitimate conflict of ownership. The question is, what shall we do about it?"

Direct, straightforward, cut right to the chase. C.J. liked that.

Apparently Lissa didn't. She let out a howl that sent shivers down C.J.'s spine. "Ragsy is *my* dog," she screeched. "Mine! Daddy, you promised, you promised—" Her face reddened as she sucked a wheezing breath. "You can't—" gasp "—let her take him—" gasp "—you can't—"

Richard sprang to his daughter's side. "Shh, punkin, no one is going to take your dog away. Deep breaths, sweetheart, take slow, deep breaths." He dug through the pocket of his sweatpants to retrieve a white plastic inhaler.

The child pushed it away, continued to wheeze until her face was suitably purple and her father's concern escalated into full-fledged fear. Only when Rags pawed her arm, whining with alarm, did the girl accept the inhaler. The attack subsided as quickly as it had begun.

Lissa hugged the tousled fur of Rags's neck, scraped C.J. with a look and made no attempt to soften a gloating grin. "Rags loves me," she purred. "He won't ever go away, 'cause he knows how sick I get when I'm sad."

C.J.'s heart sank to her toes. A manipulating child, a protective father, a shadowy specter from the past. Pain. Loneliness. Sad memories.

"Perhaps," Richard said, pocketing the inhaler and extracting a slim leather wallet, "we can come to an equitable—"

He was drowned out by Lissa's horrified shriek. "Rags, no! Come back!"

But the gleeful animal was three houses away, hot on the trail of an orange-striped cat streaking toward a neighbor's yard.

Richard dropped the wallet. "Oh, Lord. Waldo."

"Waldo?"

C.J.'s question died in chaos as the screaming child bolted after her wayward pet, ignoring shouts from her harried father. "Lissa, stop! Don't exert yourself!" He spun, stared at C.J., his face puckered with baffled annoyance that under other circumstances would have been amusing. "In six years, you couldn't have taught your dog some manners?"

With that, Richard sprinted forth to join the fray.

The orange cat, presumably the infamous Waldo, dived beneath a raised stoop. Rags followed, wriggling through the small opening and barking madly. A yowl, a hiss, a flurry of joyful woofs. An orange blur shot out from under the stoop. A shaggy mass of brown-and-white fur squeezed out, dodged Richard's grasping hands, used the stunned man's head as a springboard before dashing after the cat without so much as a backward glance at the frustrated man and the wailing child pursuing him.

It was utter pandemonium. C.J., who hadn't moved a step since the chaos began, watched with a combination of stunned disbelief and amusement that was, she supposed, wholly inappropriate for the situation. Little Lissa was clearly distraught, and her poor father was obviously as upset about his daughter's emotional state as he was about capturing the cavorting pooch.

Still, it was an amusing display of dueling wits. Rags appeared to be winning. C.J. was content to observe the comical chaos until the cat suddenly swerved toward the street with Rags still in hot pursuit. Instinctively touching two fingers to her lips, she emitted a shrill whistle.

Rags instantly skidded to a stop.

She whistled again and the animal plopped his quivering rump on the curb, staring expectantly. C.J. lifted one arm. Rags dropped to his belly. She twitched a finger. The dog rolled over. She raised her hand. He stood. She flicked her wrist. He performed a flawless back flip, then stood with his gaze focused and his tail whipping madly to await the next command.

When she touched her breastbone, Rags made a bee-line straight for her. He skidded to a stop a few feet in front of her, waited until she tapped her hip, then zipped around to "heel" position and sat smartly by her side.

"Good boy," she whispered, and was rewarded by a tongue-lolling grin.

C.J. struggled to keep her own expression impassive while the astounded dog-chasers limped back to the starting point. Lissa arrived first, her eyes enormous, followed by her father, who stared at Rags as if the animal had metamorphosed into a small, shaggy god.

C.J. cleared her throat. "Rags—" the animal gazed up adoringly "—you've behaved badly. Please apologize to Lissa and Mr. Matthews."

Rags issued two contrite whines, laid a forepaw across his muzzle.

"Good boy," she murmured, then redirected her attention. "Now, Mr. Matthews, you were saying something about manners?"

Richard paled three shades. Then and only then did C.J. allow herself the indulgence of a proud smile.

"All right, how much?"

C. J. Moray's lips slackened, then firmed. "Rags is not for sale, Mr. Matthews. I thought I'd made myself clear on that."

Richard angled a glance toward the modest home where his daughter peered out the front window with huge, tearful eyes. After exerting herself by chasing Rags, she'd suffered yet another asthma attack, after which Richard had escorted her into the house with her beloved dog, hoping he could resolve this matter logically, reasonably. Now he swallowed a twinge of panic, yanked all the currency out of his wallet and thrust it at the startled woman. "Two hundred, cash."

"Mr. Matthews—"

"If you want more, I'll have to write you a check."

C.J. extended a hand, then let it drop, shaking her head violently enough to vibrate the short, blond curls massed like golden spirals around a tanned face that he suspected was not as young as it appeared. "I know this is a difficult situation, but Rags and I...well, we have a very special relationship. Do you see that I can't give him up?"

Exquisite amber-gold eyes pleaded for understanding, understanding that Richard couldn't afford to bestow. Lissa was counting on him. "You've already given him up, Ms. Moray. Legally the animal belongs to us." He shifted, avoided the pain in those incredible golden eyes and fortified himself by angling a glance at the window behind which the child he loved more than life itself waited hopefully. "My daughter is very special, too. That dog means the world to her. It would break her heart to lose him."

"I know."

The emotion with which the words were whispered caught Richard's attention, as did the woman's obvious unhappiness at having caused his daughter grief. He studied C.J., saw the subtle droop of her shoulders, stress lines creasing her forehead, a mouth that was soft and vulnerable, lightly tinted by faint remnants of pale rose lip color.

Her clothes were casual, nondescript—a loose knit shirt, white, with short sleeves and a sports logo on the pocket, beige linen slacks and sneakers that were broken in but not quite worn-out.

His attention returned to her mouth. A flash of white as a tooth scraped her lower lip, a glimmer of pink as her tongue darted out for moisture. She cleared her throat. "I'll buy Lissa another dog, a puppy of her very own. I'll even teach her how to train it—"

"No." He flinched at his strident tone, softened it. "It's a generous offer, and I thank you for it, but Lissa won't accept another dog. She wants Rags."

"I know that, too." C.J. regarded him with peculiar sadness, and a hint of understanding that was oddly troubling. "And Lissa always gets what she wants, doesn't she?"

Richard stiffened at the truth. "My daughter is not like other children. She can't run through blooming meadows, ride her bike or play softball in the park, and she's spent more time in hospitals than most children spend in school. It's not her fault that she's fragile and ill. It's not her fault that she's doomed to grow up without her mother. It's not her fault that she has been denied the normal joys of childhood, which is all any child wants and deserves." He gritted his teeth, spoke through them. "So the answer is no, Ms. Moray, Lissa definitely does not always get what she wants."

"Please, I meant no disrespect—"

"But if you're implying that I try to compensate for all my daughter has lost by indulging those few pleasures still available to her, then I plead guilty as charged." He jammed the bills and wallet into his pocket and folded his arms, more angry at himself than the woman whose acute perception was more accurate than he cared to admit.

Richard was a father, but he wasn't a fool. He knew perfectly well that Lissa wasn't above faking illness to get her own way. His daughter could be difficult, but she had reason to be. Along with a plethora of food and environmental allergies, Lissa's asthma was a serious, sometimes life-threatening condition. The child was physically vulnerable, emotionally fragile and motherless. Despite the difficulties of single parenthood, Richard adored his child, had devoted his life to protecting her and making her happy.

At the moment, happiness hinged on the outcome of a canine custody dispute centered upon one very specific, slightly devious and undeniably clever little dog. It was a dispute Richard dared not lose.

"I'm so sorry," she murmured. Her voice was husky, like wafting wood smoke. A tingle warmed his arm where she touched him. "I know how much Lissa loves Rags, believe me, I know. But they've only been together a few weeks. Rags has spent his entire life with me. I'll give you whatever you ask for him. Five hundred...a thousand...ten thousand. I'll take out a loan, sell my car, I'll do anything." Her fingers trembled, tightened their grip above his wrist. "I know I'm a grown woman and your daughter is only a child, I know I must seem shrill and selfish, and maybe I am, but I'm desperate. You don't understand, you don't know what Rags and I have been through together.''

To his horror, tears swelled, spurted, careened down her cheeks.

''Children are resilient....'' Her voice quivered, her gaze slid to the window, behind which Lissa sobbed openly, hugging the shaggy mixed breed that consoled her with frantic face licks.

C.J. stared for a moment, then turned away, shaking her head. ''My God,'' she murmured. ''Listen to me. I can't believe that I'm actually willing to break a child's heart to protect my own.'' She wiped her face with her hands, propped one fist on her hip and stared at the ground. ''I'm sorry. I don't know what's gotten into me. There's no excuse.''

Before Richard could respond, Lissa shot out the front door, sobbing her heart out. ''No, Daddy, no, Ragsy is *my* dog! Don't let her take him away, please, please—'' gasp ''—don't let her take—'' wheeze ''—him—''

As Richard snatched out the inhaler, C.J. laid a restraining hand on his arm as she squatted down in front of the wheezing, red-faced child. ''I'm not going to take your dog away,'' she said quietly. ''But there are some things about Rags you need to know. If you love him as much as I think you do, you'll calm down now, so you can listen and learn how to take good care of him.''

To Richard's shock, the strained gasps ceased, the child's breathing deepened as she focused a skeptical stare. ''I already take good care of Rags.''

''I'm sure you do, but did you know, for example, that Rags loves bananas?'' The girl's eyes widened. ''That's right, but if he eats more than two bites, he gets really,

really sick, so you have to be sure to keep them out of reach. He likes apples, too, but again, you have to be careful how much he can have. There are certain brands of dog food he won't eat.''

The girl brightened. "Daddy had to buy three different kinds before he found one Rags liked.''

"You see? You've already discovered one of his secrets. He's finicky, and as long as you feed him apples and bananas, he figures he doesn't have to bother with stuff he doesn't really like. You have to be careful only to give him treats that are good for him. His tummy can be sensitive.''

Lissa nodded solemnly. "Is he allergic, like me?''

"Well, he reacts badly to fleabites, I'm afraid, but that can be controlled. I have some medicine that helps him. I'll—'' She paused, bit her lip, then managed a tremulous smile. "I'll bring it to you.''

The child cocked her head. "You will?''

"Yes. I'll bring you all of his vet records, and his favorite toys, too, but you have to promise me that you'll watch him carefully, especially when he's on his skateboard, because sometimes he doesn't pay attention to—''

Richard interrupted. "Skateboard?''

C.J. glanced up with a shaky smile that made his heart quiver strangely. "Rags is quite the little sports dog. He also jumps rope, surfs and knows how to ride a windjammer. I was planning to take hang gliding lessons this summer, and had a special harness made so he could come with me....'' Her voice drifted away.

Lissa's eyes were appreciatively wide. "Gee, Rags does lots of tricks, doesn't he?''

"Yes.'' It was a whisper. C.J. cleared her throat, offered a bright smile with quivering corners. "But he can also be quite a rascal. He'll try to get away with lots of things that are dangerous. You'll have to learn how to protect him, and keep him safe. You have to train him to respond to you. I can teach you how, if you like."

It was a generous offer. For a moment, Richard thought Lissa might actually accept. Instead, the child's eyes narrowed with suspicion.

"I can do it all by myself." Lissa spun, strode to the front door, paused with a triumphant gleam in her eyes. "Ragsy is *my* dog. He doesn't need you anymore."

"Lissa!" Richard flinched as the front door slammed, then faced the shaken woman rising to her feet. "I'm sorry."

C.J. shrugged. "It's all right. This has been difficult for her. I understand." Oddly enough, he believed that she did. She raked a hand through her hair, took a deep breath, then suddenly fumbled in her slacks pocket and extracted a business card. "I'll forward Rags's things. If you have any questions or problems, you can reach me here."

He absently glanced at the card, did a double take. "'All That Jazz Academy of Dance'?"

"If I'm not there, that number will forward to my beeper."

She licked her lips, blinked rapidly. Too rapidly. "Please give my regards to Lissa. Tell her I'm glad Rags found such a good home."

"Ms. Moray—"

But she'd spun away, crossed the yard and was already climbing into her car. A moment later, she drove down the street and disappeared, leaving Richard both relieved and conflicted.

For the sake of a child she did not even know, C. J. Moray had relinquished all claim to the pet she clearly adored. He was grateful, of course, but he was also deeply saddened by the niggling sense that this might have been one battle his daughter should not have won.

"You just *left* him there?" Under the best of circumstances Bobbi Macafee was an imposing woman, tall, broad shouldered, with a thick mane of ebony hair and a horsey face that oddly enough was not unattractive. When perturbed, that face tightened into a furious mask, reddened like a neon beet and was frightening enough to have once cowed a professional wrestler, who'd unwisely refused to pose for a photograph, into hiding behind his trainer to escape her wrath.

Now Bobbi loomed large and intimidating, jammed her fists on her hips and gaped at C.J. as if she'd just confessed to abandoning an infant on a doorstep. "How could you do such a thing? I mean, Rags is *family!* You might as well have given up your own child!"

"There wasn't any choice," C.J. mumbled, retrieving the palm-sized glucometer from a kitchen shelf. She pricked her finger, smeared a blood drop on a test strip, which she inserted into a slot at the side of the machine. "That little girl loves Rags. She would have been devastated to lose him."

"What about you?" Bobbi insisted. "Don't your feelings count?"

"I'm a grown-up. She's a child, a sick, lonely little girl who desperately needs love." C.J. checked the digital readout for her blood sugar level, then put the glucometer away, measured a precise amount of orange juice into a glass and prepared a lean turkey sandwich for lunch.

Behind her Bobbi paced and fumed, ranting about the injustice of the world. C.J. ignored her. Although fiercely loyal and opinionated to the point of irksome, Bobbi was first and foremost a dear friend. They were like sisters, had been since their college days, and C.J. understood that the guilt of having been responsible for Rags's loss in the first place weighed heavily on her roommate's conscience.

Not that C.J. blamed her. Moving an entire household wasn't easy, even for a woman who could bench-press two hundred pounds without breaking a sweat. It wasn't Bobbi's fault she'd been left to tackle the task alone. If anyone was responsible for Rags's loss, it was C.J. herself. She should have been there to protect her precious pet during the move.

"You should sue," Bobbi announced, nodding so vigorously that her spectacles slipped down her nose. "I know a lawyer—"

"No."

"But the county was negligent! Honest to God, Ceejz, I called the shelter six times a day for two solid weeks after Rags ran away, and every dadgummed time they said no animal of that description had been picked up. They lied, they screwed up, they gave your dog away, for Pete's sake! Someone has to be held accountable for that."

Heaving a sigh, C.J. set the orange juice down. "No lawyers, no lawsuits. It's over. I've made my decision.

Rags is happy, well cared for, and loved. Please, can't we drop it now? This entire subject is…painful.''

Bobbi's face crumpled in despair. ''Oh, hon—'' She stepped forward, stopped when C.J. raised a palm to signal that she was perfectly fine and didn't wish to be fussed over.

Of course, C.J. wasn't perfectly fine and Bobbi clearly knew that. She also understood C.J.'s aversion to being the subject of worry or concern, and respected her silent request even if her furrowed brow displayed disagreement with it.

Frustrated, Bobbi straightened her glasses, heaved a deflating sigh. ''Look, I have to go. The magazine is sending me out to interview an over-the-hill jockey who's accusing some racing association of age discrimination.''

C.J. nodded without comment, took a bite of sandwich while her roommate hustled around the cluttered room gathering her briefcase, pocket recorder, camera and other tools of the journalistic trade.

Pausing at the front door, Bobbi shouldered the briefcase strap, raked red-tipped fingers through her thick tangle of long black hair and regarded her friend with blatant concern. ''Are you going to be all right, Ceejz? I can reschedule this thing—''

''I'm fine,'' C.J. assured her. ''You go, do your job.'' She enforced that edict with the brightest smile she could muster, and tipped the orange juice glass in salute. ''Knock 'em dead, tiger.''

Bobbi responded with a thin nod, an even thinner smile, then slipped out the door.

Alone now, C.J. slumped against the kitchen counter, forcing herself to finish the tasteless sandwich. Eating was more ritual than pleasure. Her body required food whether she wanted it or not. At the moment, her stomach twisted, her head hurt and she was angry with herself for being so emotional.

The reunion with her beloved pet had been bittersweet. Although deeply grateful that Rags was alive and happy, the emptiness in her heart seemed suddenly overwhelming again. For the past six years that crafty canine had been her constant companion, from romps on the ski slope to ocean surfing excursions, and had even shared a hot-air balloon trip she and Bobbi had taken to research one of her roommate's magazine articles.

Rags was the only creature on earth who accepted C.J.'s quirks without question. He never criticized, never furrowed a doggy brow with worry, never gave scolded warnings or repeated medication reminders. He was thirty fur-covered pounds of unconditional love and acceptance that C.J. desperately needed.

But little Lissa needed it more.

The Matthews child had put a mirror to C.J.'s own lonely childhood, a poignant reminder of how much a friend—even a shaggy canine friend—means to a sick and lonely little girl.

Since C.J. wouldn't—couldn't—take that away, she set about fulfilling her promise to forward Rags's possessions. Retrieving a box from her bedroom closet, she examined the contents. Tiny tags, still snugged on Rags's collar ring; his old training collar and leash; special ointment for the skin condition that flared occasionally, along with a folder of medical records, all meticulously maintained from the day she'd brought him home as a feisty ten-week-old pup; his favorite chew toys, the plastic Frisbee he adored; a tiny wet suit for beach excursions, a warm saddle coat for snow trips; and of course, his beloved skateboard.

There were photographs, too, a record of their time together, of the adventures they'd shared. But the pictures were hers, and hers alone. All she had left were those images, and the memories they evoked. Good memories. Joyful memories.

Memories of mountain hikes and walks in the park, of the reassuring bed lump that always crowded her legs, of the rushed vet visit when a wasp had stung his tongue.

Memories of warm fur and a cold nose and wet, doggy kisses that made her sputter and laugh. Memories of friendship. Memories of love.

C.J. remembered it all, relived it all. And she smiled through her tears, content in the knowledge that there would be more memories of friendship and love created between a big-hearted pooch and the lonely little girl who needed him.

Chapter Two

"I can have the revisions done by the end of the week." Shifting the telephone, Richard spread the curled blueprint over his drafting table, readjusted the corner tape to hold it flat. "The changes you're suggesting shouldn't have more than a minimal impact on cost—"

"Daddy!"

"But I'll run the new specs through the computer and give you an update—"

"Daa-ddy!"

"In a day or so." Richard sighed as Lissa stomped into the secluded den that served as his architectural office. "Listen, Jay, can I get back to you on this? Thanks."

"Ragsy won't play with me," Lissa announced as soon as he'd cradled the receiver. "He won't play dress-up or chase his ball or do anything 'cept sit on the back of Gramps's chair with that dumb Frisbee in his mouth and look out the window."

Richard swiveled on his drafting stool, and squeezed the back of his aching neck. As he opened his mouth to speak, one of a half-dozen antique clocks displayed throughout the office began to chime the half hour. Seconds later another chimed in, then another. The sound soothed Richard, offered a moment of calm retreat. He loved clocks, particularly the old ones, with rich embellishments, gilded etchings and intricate carvings crafted by long-ago artists who took pride in their work. His collection of such treasures was a source of great joy to him, and he could spend hours restoring a neglected piece to its original luster.

After a few seconds, the clocks fell silent, and Richard returned his attention to the sulking child beside his drafting stool. His voice was firm, but not particularly convincing. "Lissa, you know you're not supposed to interrupt me while I'm working."

She poked her lip out, folded her arms. "I want to play with Rags."

Heaving a frustrated sigh, Richard motioned his daughter over, pulled her into his lap. "Rags doesn't want to play right now, punkin. He's feeling sad."

Lissa's lip quivered, then clamped in anger. "It's that mean lady's fault. Gramps even said so."

With some effort, Richard kept an impassive expression. Thompson McCade was rich, powerful, smoothly controlling and as devoted to his grandchild as was the man's timid, beleaguered wife. Richard considered his father-in-law a tyrannical bully, but had always kept that opinion to himself out of respect for his wife's memory, and because he didn't want to alienate Lissa from her grandparents' love and attention.

Now, as always, Richard tried to straddle a fine line between supporting McCade's inappropriate blame-mongering, and openly contradicting his daughter's beloved Gramps. "I can understand your grandfather's concern, punkin. He hates to see you upset. But you have to remember that Gramps hasn't met Ms. Moray, so he's really not in a position to comment on her motives. I believe she only wants what's best for Rags, and for you, too."

"I don't care. I hate her."

"That's not a nice thing to say."

"Well, I do hate her, I do. She's trying to steal my dog and I just wish she'd dry up and die."

"That's enough." Speaking sternly enough to startle his daughter into attention, Richard enforced his position. "It's okay for you to feel bad, and it's okay for you to be angry, but it's not okay for you to say mean things about people even when they're not around to hear them."

"But it's not fair," Lissa wailed. "Ragsy is *my* dog." Pulling away from her father's embrace, the child leapt down, kicked at a cardboard blueprint tube lying beside the drafting table. "He was real happy before she showed up, and now he won't eat or play or do anything at all. He's no fun anymore, and it's *all her fault.*"

After emphasizing her pique with another kick at the hapless mailing tube, Lissa spun on her heel and marched out. A moment later, her bedroom door slammed.

Richard pushed away the contract file with which he'd been working, leaned back on his stool and rubbed his eyelids until they stung. As annoyed as he was with his father-in-law's interference, he still couldn't blame Lissa for feeling helpless and frustrated, particularly when he felt that way himself.

Ever since C. J. Moray's less than fortuitous appearance, Rags had shown every symptom of an animal grieving himself sick. The poor little dog had eaten nothing for four days now, and even the neatly packed box of toys, bowls and other doggy belongings that had mysteriously arrived on the front porch hadn't helped dissuade the animal's melancholy mood. If anything, the pooch seemed even sadder, carrying the pathetic Frisbee in his mouth as he wandered from room to room, then returned to his vigil at the front window and stared dolefully outside as if awaiting his mistress's return.

Yesterday Richard had decided a romp in the neighborhood park would perk Rags up. The moment the front door opened, the dog had shot to the very spot in the front yard where C. J. Moray had been standing, then followed her scent to the curb. Had the animal not been leashed, there was no doubt in Richard's mind that Rags would have chased the scent as far as possible in pursuit of the mistress he had never forgotten, and still clearly adored.

Rags was obviously heartbroken. Richard feared the stoic little pooch would grieve himself to death, and was convinced that something had to be done. He'd already formulated a plan. Lissa wouldn't like it, of course.

But she'd like the alternative even less.

The dance studio was situated in a tidy corner of a bustling strip mall, the kind where neighborhood residents gathered for groceries, a quick video rental, or to peruse the aisles of a local bookstore. Richard parked, paused outside the studio's glass front to read a few posted flyers announcing beginning ballet lessons, tap dance classes and the like.

He swallowed a guilty twinge. Lissa had always wanted to take ballet lessons. The request had been denied, as had her desire to participate in playground softball and other such athletic endeavors, because Richard was worried such physical exertion would exacerbate her asthma.

Lissa's asthma was no joke. She'd nearly died twice, and had been hospitalized more times than Richard could count. Doctors hoped the condition would ease as she matured, but so far there'd been no perceptible improvement. Attacks came on suddenly, without warning, and could escalate to life-threatening proportions with hideous speed. It was a terrifying situation, not for the faint of heart.

Lissa's mother hadn't been able to deal with the terror, the helpless horror of watching her only child slip to the edge of death time and time and time again. Richard had understood his wife's fear. He'd even understood her guilt, and the secret sense of failure at having given birth to a frail and sickly child. What Richard hadn't understood, still couldn't understand, was why a mother, any mother, would give up on her own child by giving up on herself.

Despite years of emotional withdrawal during which Richard and his wife had become virtual strangers, he'd been nonetheless shattered by her death.

Now he gazed into the glass window, his own reflection revealing the bitterness of that memory. It hurt. It would always hurt. He'd failed as a husband. He was determined not to fail as a father.

Squaring his shoulders, he yanked open the dance-studio door and walked into chaos.

Beyond the partitioned entry, blaring music vibrated the walls, the floor and his back molars. Bongos bonged, cymbals crashed, tambourines tonated in a wild calypso cantata that was part Caribbean reggae and part "Dance of the Sugar Plum Fairies," with a jarring jab of New Orleans jazz tossed in for good measure.

Richard would have hocked everything he owned for a sturdy set of earplugs.

Above the deafening musical fray was a voice, sharp, firm and familiar. "And one and two...twirl, twirl... hands high, Shelly, reach for the sky...that's good, very good. And bend, twist, and bend and twist...come on, fairies, high on your toes, stretch those arms...fluid, graceful, hands flutter like fairy wings."

Sidling along the partition, Richard chanced a peek into the heart of the bustling studio, where over a dozen exuberant youngsters pirouetted through choreographed routines. In the center, a sleek blonde in black leotards accented by a hot-pink-and-fuchsia thong darted around the dancers, clapping rhythm with her hands and occasionally pausing to straighten a child's saggy shoulder, or lift a droopy chin.

To Richard's astonishment, the blond instructor paused in the center of the melee, where a young girl in a wheelchair extended swaying arms in the air. "Marty, Susan, take Shelly's chair now and turn slowly, slowly.... Shelly, hon, keep those arms high, hands graceful...that's wonderful!" The instructor clapped quickly now, increasing the pace. "The dragon is coming, the dragon is coming! Fairies leap, leap, drop to a crouch. Shelly, cower in fear...turn the chair faster, girls, faster, faster...that's it, terrific...."

She spun toward the sidelines, where a rhythm section of youngsters perched anxiously on the edge of their seats clutching a variety of tambourines, shakers and bongo drums. "Dragon is—" she pointed at a pale boy with a pair of cymbals held at the ready *"—here!"*

The youngster slammed his cymbals together with a proud, gap-toothed grin.

"Curtain!" The instructor threw up her arms as the music ceased abruptly. "Wonderful class, you were all just perfect!"

A din of happy voices erupted as children scampered—or rolled—toward a scatter of adults, presumably proud parents, seated in a makeshift gallery of folding chairs surrounding a refreshment table. The rhythm section dropped their instruments, blasted across the room to attack the cookie-and-juice buffet with gusto appropriate to a pack of sweaty, starving prepubescents.

And in the center of bustling activity, C. J. Moray dabbed her face with a towel, listening to the excited ramblings of a small, dark-haired princess who was apparently so enthused by her own performance that she felt compelled to review each step of it in painful detail. Ms. Moray listened as if raptly fascinated, offering affirmative nods and bright smiles that left the little girl puffed with pride, and clearly thrilled.

Under other circumstances the child's joy would have been mesmerizing, but it was the woman upon whom Richard's attention was riveted. Her face was flushed and glowing, with damp blond tendrils clinging to her cheeks likes strands of gleaming gold. Eyes like sparkling amber wine, a smile bright as a sun-drenched rose garden, a laugh so husky and melodic that it warmed his blood and sent chills marching down his spine at the same time.

Richard couldn't take his eyes off her.

Suddenly her smile hesitated, her eyes clouded. A pucker of sensation touched her brow. She looked up, met his gaze, held it. Time stopped. A minute. Two. Ten. He didn't know, didn't care. For those moments, those indefinable instants of eternity, nothing else existed but this woman, this incredibly beautiful woman whose mesmerizing gaze sucked the breath from his body, drained the reason from his mind.

He was aware of her subtle movement, noticed when she touched the child's shoulder, murmured something that sent the girl scampering happily away. He knew he should do something, say something, but was rooted in place, helpless as an insect pinned to a corkboard.

She studied him a moment longer, then draped the towel around her neck, glided toward him so gracefully he wondered if her feet actually touched the floor. The leotard left nothing to the imagination, revealing a swell of round breasts, a sleek torso with hips that rolled smoothly as she moved, legs long and strong enough to wrap a man's body and lift him straight to heaven.

A smile touched her lips, lush lips, devoid of artificial color yet naturally pink, pearlescent, enticingly moist. The lips moved. "Mr. Matthews, what a pleasant surprise."

Richard wanted to respond. He really did. His brain told his mouth to speak, commanded it to do so, but there must have been some kind of short circuit, because to his horror he felt his head jerk in a cruel caricature of a nod.

She cocked her head, regarded him with a mixture of amusement and anxiety. "Is there something I can do for you?"

"Yes." The word slid out on a breath, the poignant sigh of a lovestruck adolescent. He coughed, cleared his throat and yanked his gaze away, concentrating on the pandemonium of scampering youngsters until he felt the peculiar numbness seep from his mind. "This is not what I expected."

She studied him a moment more, then followed his gaze. "It's a little crazier than usual. Things get wild the week before a recital."

He chose not to correct her errant assumption that he'd been referring to the dance class rather than his unanticipated physiological response. "I'm surprised at the, er, variety of participants."

"We try to integrate special needs children in our regular dance classes. Shelly—" she nodded toward the laughing child in the wheelchair "—was born with a spinal defect. She can't walk, but as you may have noticed, she's an excellent dancer."

"She did seem to be enjoying herself."

"But—?"

He chanced a look, recognized the question in her eyes. "I'll admit I was surprised to see how well the other children accepted her."

"Unless taught otherwise, children are naturally accepting of people's differences. Besides, many of our students have limitations of one kind or another, although they might not be as noticeable as Shelly's. Donna, for example—'' she nodded toward a tall girl wearing a colorful paisley scarf ''—is undergoing chemotherapy. The treatment saps her strength, so we've choreographed a part for her that requires minimal stamina and endurance. That way she can continue to participate with her friends, and isn't made to feel different.''

"But she *is* different," Richard noted, stunned that the girl's parents would allow such strenuous activity. "She's a very sick child."

"Yes, she is." C.J. grasped the towel hem with both hands, shifted her stance to angle a sideways glance at Richard. "Even sick children need to belong. They need friends, and fun, and the joy of accomplishment."

"They need care and treatment." The response was more forceful than intended, although C.J. neither flinched nor disputed it.

"I require a medical release from all my students," she said. "If a child has special needs, I consult with his or her physician on a lesson plan that is within medical guidelines." Snapping the draped towel, she suddenly spun to face him with a gaze so acute he squirmed at its intensity. "But I suspect you didn't drive all the way across town to discuss dance lessons."

"Ah, no."

Her eyes widened. "Is Rags all right? Oh, God, the skateboard. There's been an accident, hasn't there? Is it bad?" She flung the towel away, dashed to a coatrack in the foyer. "Where is he, what vet hospital do you use—?"

"There hasn't been an accident." Richard caught up with her at the front door, grasped her elbow as she was struggling into her jacket. "Rags is fine."

Her arms fell limp, her eyes filled with relieved moisture. "He's not hurt?"

"No."

She touched her face, closed her eyes. "Thank God."
A shuddering sigh, a moment to compose herself, then
she squared her shoulders, cast him a curious glance.
"Then why are you here?"

"Well, it does have to do with Rags, I'm afraid. Is
there somewhere we could talk?"

Behind the closed doors of the tiny, cluttered office
that had once been a janitorial closet, C.J. rested a hip
on the edge of her wobbly desk, and frowned. "Let me
get this straight, you're offering me joint custody of
Rags?"

"Not exactly." Richard jerked as the folding chair
shifted, then leaned forward, planting his hands on his
knees as if preparing to leap should the unsteady seating
device suddenly collapse. "More precisely, I'm suggesting a visitation arrangement, specific schedules whereby
you and Rags could, er, spend time together."

"And you're doing this out of the goodness of your
heart?"

He appeared stung by the inference. "Contrary to popular belief, I am not utterly devoid of feelings. Clearly,
you're fond of the animal and he, likewise, is fond of
you." His gaze darted, and the subtle slide of presumably
damp palms over his slacks did not escape notice. "A
change in ownership is traumatic for any pet. I thought
regular visits might lessen his anxiety."

C.J. nodded. "Rags has stopped eating, hasn't he?"

Richard deflated before her eyes. "Yes."

"How long?"

"Four days."

She sucked a shocked breath, let the air out with a hiss. "*Four days?* Why didn't you tell me?"

"I'm telling you now." His gaze narrowed. "Has he done this sort of thing before?"

She nodded absently, chewed her lip. "It's his way of pouting."

"You could have warned me."

Flinching at the reproach, C.J. offered a limp shrug. "It didn't occur to me. I mean, he'd already been with you for weeks and there hadn't been a problem." She raked her hair, wished the office was large enough for her to pace. "When can I see him?"

Richard stood, smoothed the suit coat that made him look considerably more dapper than the saggy jogging suit he'd worn over the weekend. She had to admit he'd cleaned up nicely. Very nicely.

He offered a brusque nod. "You can see him whenever it's convenient."

"My last class ends at six. I could be at your place by half-past." When another curt nod indicated the timing was acceptable, C.J. broached a more sensitive subject. "What does Lissa think of this arrangement?"

With a pained shrug, he shifted to avoid her gaze. "Lissa loves Rags. She will do what is best for him."

As he reached for the doorknob, C.J. touched his wrist. Her fingertips brushed bare skin, tingled at a tickle of soft hair. "Thank you," she whispered.

His eyes darkened, black pupils expanding inside a ring of soft heather sage. For a long moment he said nothing, simply stared with an intensity that left her breathless. Then he blinked, nodded, opened the door and was gone.

C.J. stood there, vaguely aware that her knees were trembling. She touched her mouth, transferred the tingling from her fingertips to her lips. In a sense, it was their very first kiss. It would not, she decided, be their last.

Woman-and-dog reunion part *deux* was every bit as exuberant and joyful as the first had been. Rags shot out the front door barking madly, leapt into C.J.'s arms and covered her face with familiar wet kisses. C.J. laughed and sputtered, hugged his wriggling body so tightly it was a wonder the poor animal's eyes didn't bulge.

Richard Matthews watched from the open doorway with a peculiar look on his face, while his clearly heartbroken daughter stared through the front window with wide and haunting eyes. The image was pitifully sad and sobering.

C.J. gave Rags another hug, then whispered, "Go get your Frisbee." The dog leapt down, dashed between Richard's legs and disappeared into the house. Although C.J. spoke to Richard, she couldn't take her eyes off the tearful child in the window. "I thought I'd take him for a run in the park, if that's all right."

"That's fine," Richard murmured, but C.J. wasn't listening. She was mesmerized by Lissa's pale face, the small, quivering mouth and eyes filled with yearning for a childhood denied her.

Just as childhood had once been denied another young girl. Images of the past marched through her memory, a thoughtful reflection of that other lonely youngster who'd watched from a sickroom window as her father and siblings played ball in the front yard. She remembered the pain, the longing, the resentment that festered into fury. She remembered the rage, the uncontrollable anger lashing out at those she'd loved the most.

Most of all, she remembered the loneliness.

Because C.J.'s own childhood, like little Lissa's, had been one of isolation, medication and excessive parental protection. It had been a loving prison, but a prison nonetheless, and she'd spent her adult years overcoming— some would say overcompensating for all those lonely years and lost adventures.

Now C.J. saw herself in the reflection of the sad child behind the window. She understood how it felt to read terror in a parent's eyes, to be shunned by other children. To be different.

She knew, she understood and her heart broke for that lonely little girl. And for this one.

"It is an outrage." Clearly furious, Thompson McCade tapped the bowl of his pipe on a crystal ashtray. "You disappoint me, Richard."

"I did what was necessary."

"Necessary?" The imposing man strode across the room, seated himself in the extravagant recliner that he'd claimed as his own, and bit down on the stem of the unlit pipe so hard his teeth clicked. He fumed a moment before removing the pipe and cradling the unlit bowl in his palm. "Since when is it necessary to put the superficial desires of a stranger above the needs of your own child? Allissa is devastated by your callous disregard of her feelings, Richard, and quite frankly, so am I. Melinda would be horrified—''

"That's enough," Richard said quietly, although his jaw twitched in warning.

A vein pulsed on McCade's forehead. "How dare you speak to me like that? Melinda was my daughter, my only child—''

"She was my wife." With some effort, Richard unfurled his fisted fingers, reminded himself that his daughter was in the kitchen with her grandmother, close enough to overhear. He lowered his voice. "I've asked you before, and I'm asking you again to refrain from using Lissa's mother as a club with which to beat me into submission each and every time we have a disagreement. I'm perfectly willing to listen to your opinions, Thompson, but Lissa is my daughter, and I will make the final decision as to what is or is not in her best interest."

A flush of red fury crawled from McCade's beefy neck to a face flexing with indignation. He was an impressive man, barrel-chested and large in stature, with a thick shock of gunmetal gray hair and a bulbous nose that would have been clownish if not for the piercing, pitiless intensity of eyes that demanded respect, but rarely bestowed it. Thompson McCade was not accustomed to argument. He was a man to be reckoned with, ruthless, relentless and powerful.

He was also a royal pain in the butt.

"I've made my decision," Richard repeated calmly. "Either Lissa learns to share her pet, or she'll have to give him up entirely. The choice is hers."

"That is grossly unfair." McCade's face darkened to a worrisome purple. "I won't allow it."

Richard heaved a weary shrug, chose not to point out that when it came to this home and this family, McCade was not in a position to allow or disallow anything. The older man clearly understood that, although ego prevented him from acknowledging any limitation of the power upon which his entire self-image had been built.

So Richard let his father-in-law sputter and rant without contradiction. He didn't agree with the man's point of view, but he didn't exactly disagree with it, either.

In truth, Richard didn't care for the current situation any more than McCade. He loved his daughter dearly, understood how wounded she was by her pet's affection for the athletic blonde with a pocket full of dog biscuits and a boisterous laugh that McCade would most certainly label as bohemian. Richard hated to see his child so unhappy, but he certainly couldn't disregard the needs of a helpless animal. It wasn't Rags's fault that Lissa was overindulged and selfish. In a sense, it wasn't Lissa's fault, either. Richard blamed himself.

"Daddy?"

Richard blinked, turned just as Lissa scampered from the kitchen to clamber into her grandfather's lap.

She beamed hopefully. "Do I get Rags back, Daddy, do I, huh, do I?"

From the corner of his eye he saw Sarah McCade hovering shyly in the kitchen doorway, wringing her wrinkled hands. "Of course you get Rags back, punkin, just as soon as Ms. Moray returns from the park."

"Then I won't ever have to share him again, right, Daddy?"

Richard sighed as McCade's eyes narrowed in warning. "We've already been through this, Lissa. Ms. Moray will be visiting with Rags two evenings a week, and have him all day Saturday.''

Horrified, the child spun on her grandfather's lap. ''But you promised, Gramps, you promised that you'd make Daddy give me my dog back.''

To Richard's surprise, Sarah McCade, who rarely said anything beyond ''good morning,'' and even then felt guilty about verbalizing the observation, suddenly stepped forward. ''Sweetheart, we talked about this in the kitchen. You don't want your doggy to be sad or sick, do you?''

The child's chin jutted stubbornly. Tears leaked from her eyes. ''Gramps *promised.*'' A small wheeze, then a louder one followed by an interminable, rasping gasp.

Richard nearly moaned aloud.

''Look what you've done,'' McCade boomed. ''Now she's having an attack. Sarah, get the child's medication.''

The woman hovered frantically before dashing off to do her husband's bidding. She'd barely left the room when her gasping granddaughter glimpsed a familiar form dashing across the front yard. ''Rags!'' the child shouted, then leapt from her grandfather's lap and shot across the room, her asthma attack instantly and miraculously abated. She yanked open the front door, clapping gleefully. ''Rags, Rags!''

The animal literally flew through the door, greeted Lissa with a series of joyous kisses, then dashed into the kitchen. Lissa ran after him, nearly knocking into her bewildered grandmother, who'd just emerged clutching the child's inhaler.

Richard stood, offered his mother-in-law a thin smile.

"Thank you, Sarah, but apparently Lissa is feeling much better now."

On cue, Lissa leaned out of the doorway with an exploding grin. "Rags is eating, Daddy, he's gobbling up everything in his dish!"

"That's nice, punkin," Richard murmured, distracted by the breathless woman hovering in the doorway with a grass-stained Frisbee clutched in one hand. He took a step toward her, jerked to a stop as Sarah McCade hurried past, gushing.

"You must be Ms. Moray," she murmured, pumping the startled woman's free hand. "I'm so happy to meet you. I'm Lissa's grandmother—"

"Sarah!" McCade boomed.

The woman flushed, fell silent, backed away clasping her hands as McCade studied C. J. Moray with undisguised contempt. "So you're the one." There was no mistaking the disdain in his voice.

To her credit, C.J. cocked her head as though sizing the older man up, then offered a smile that was somehow sincere and cautious at the same time. "You must be Lissa's grandfather. I'm pleased to meet you."

Richard stepped between them before McCade could say something even more blatantly rude. Cupping C.J.'s elbow, he ushered her to the porch. "I'm sorry about that. I wish I could tell you that beneath that gruff exterior beats a heart of gold, but the only thing beneath that gruff exterior is a gruff interior."

Her laugh was soft, smoky. Enticing. "I understand."

For some odd reason, he believed her. "Thank you."

"For what?"

"For everything." He was mesmerized by her smile,

hypnotized by the amused sparkle in her dark eyes. This was without doubt the most intoxicating woman he'd ever laid eyes on. She was also the most perceptive, a thought that was soon to be proven yet again as she gazed past his shoulder.

The sparkle drained from her eyes, replaced by a tender warmth that was, oddly enough, even more alluring. "Hello, Lissa. It's nice to see you again."

With some effort Richard followed her gaze, saw his daughter on the porch looking sullen and angry. She jerked a thumb at the Frisbee C.J. held. "Leave that here," she commanded. "It belongs to Rags."

Still smiling, C.J. held the Frisbee out until Lissa stomped down the steps to retrieve it. "Is Rags the first dog you've owned?"

Lissa paused, issued a sharp nod that was more an expression of annoyance than agreement.

"Pets can be difficult, can't they?" Lowering herself, C.J. sat on her heels so her face and the child's were on the same level. "Having a dog is kind of like having a naughty child and an irritating kid brother all at the same time. Except, of course, my irritating kid brother never drank out of the toilet. At least, I don't think so. He *was* pretty weird."

Despite an obvious intent to remain angry, Lissa couldn't prevent a smile from tweaking the corners of her tightly clamped mouth. "Do you have lots of brothers?"

"Two, one older than me and one younger. I also have two older sisters."

"You musta had lots of fun playing and stuff."

"Yes, we had fun. Sometimes we hurt each other's

feelings and made each other mad, but we never really meant to." She paused a beat before adding, "Just like Rags never meant to hurt your feelings or make you mad. He loves you very much."

The child's lip quivered. "Then how come he wants to go play with you?"

"Because he loves me, too. Dogs have room in their hearts to love lots of people."

"Uh-uh." A look of disbelief.

"It's true, cross my heart." She drew an invisible *X* on her chest, flashed a dazzling smile. "You love Rags, don't you?"

Lissa sniffed, nodded.

"And you love your daddy, too, just like you love your grandpa and your grandma?" C.J. waited for the child's limp shrug. "How would you feel if someone told you that you had to choose only one of them to love, and you weren't allowed to care about anyone else ever again?"

Another limp shrug. "Bad."

"Of course you'd feel bad, but even more important, you wouldn't be able to do it." C.J. hesitated, then took the child's hand, sandwiched it between her own palms. "You couldn't stop loving your daddy or your grandparents just because someone told you to, and Rags can't stop caring about me, either, but that doesn't mean he loves you any less."

To Richard's astonishment, Lissa bent to whisper something in C.J.'s ear. The child smiled, then laughed. A moment later the two females were giggling madly, whispering like old chums. If he hadn't seen it with his own eyes, he wouldn't have believed it. His sullen, selfish child was engrossed in clearly joyful conversation with the very same woman she'd demonized only moments ago.

C.J. stood suddenly, skimmed a glance at Richard. "Rags and I are taking a nature hike on Saturday. Would it be all right if Lissa came along? You're welcome, too, of course."

"Please, Daddy? I wanna go, I really, really do. Please?"

Richard's initial instinct was to refuse. Outings with Lissa were difficult, tension-filled affairs that must be tediously prepared for with medical precision. Still, there was something fascinating about C. J. Moray, her vibrancy and infectious zest for life, the ease with which she'd transformed his sulking daughter into a happy, hopeful child.

"Absolutely not!" Thompson McCade loomed in the doorway, red faced and furious. "I will not have my granddaughter traipsing through muck and mud until her lungs explode. I will not allow it."

All doubts dissipated instantly. If McCade was dead set against something, then Richard was dead set in favor of it. He met his father-in-law's angry stare with one of cold determination, but it was C.J. to whom he spoke. "What time Saturday?"

"Ah, is eight too early?"

"Eight is perfect," Richard replied tightly. "We'll be ready."

Lissa whooped. McCade blustered. C.J. smiled.

And for the first time in more years than he could remember, Richard was looking forward to the weekend.

Chapter Three

"**G**ood Lord, what on earth is that?"

Richard hoisted the stuffed duffel into the back of his minivan. "Just a few things Lissa might need."

"Where's the kitchen sink?" C.J. asked with a smile. "She'll have to wash up after the exertion of hauling a hundred-pound load up a dusty canyon trail."

"No sink," he murmured seriously. "Just a portable shower." Grabbing a red-and-white cooler from the curb, he positioned it beside the duffel, then studied the load, trying to think what he'd forgotten. Allergy medications, anaphylactic shock kit, special liquid wash to remove poison oak sap and other potential skin irritants, two bottles of refill medication for her inhaler— Oh, Lord. The inhaler.

Richard frantically patted his empty breast pocket, then dug into his slacks, relaxing slightly when he located the item in his left pants pocket.

"Is there ice in the cooler?"

"Hmm?" He glanced over just as C.J. slid a silver-hued, insulated pack the size of a shoebox into the van. A clear plastic food container was tucked under her arm. "Yes, there's ice in it. Do you want to put that inside?"

She handed the container over. "Is there enough room?"

"We'll make room." Opening the cooler, Richard moved a few soda cans, situated it atop a bed of ice. "You didn't have to bring your own lunch. We have plenty of food."

"I always bring my own munchies," she murmured, shading her eyes. "I brought a cooler, too, but it's full. I guess I got a little carried away with the bottled water. Rags likes his Evian chilled."

"The dog drinks designer water?"

"It's a weakness." She disappeared in front of the van, where her own tiny compact was parked, returned a moment later with several towels tucked under her arm, another cooler that was smaller than Richard's, but almost as heavy.

He loaded the remaining supplies into the van while C.J. glanced toward the house, where Lissa and Rags were tussling in the front yard. She called out. "Lissa, would you mind getting Rags's leash…oh, and could you bring his water bowl, and that floaty rubber doughnut thingy with the flowers on it? It's his favorite swim toy. And don't forget his Frisbee."

To Richard's shock, Lissa scrambled to her feet with a cheery "Okay," and dashed into the house.

"How'd you do that?"

C.J. glanced over her shoulder. "Do what?"

"Lissa rarely does anything remotely resembling a chore without argument."

"Oh, that." She shrugged. "Lissa understands that Rags is depending on her. Responsibility is a marvelous teacher."

"Responsibility? She's only eight years old."

C.J. regarded him for a moment, then glanced away with a mysterious smile. "One is never too young for love, Mr. Matthews—"

"Richard."

She quirked a brow, widened her smile. "Richard." Her gaze deepened, softened. "As I was saying, love brings out the best in people, even very small people. The happiness and well-being of those we love becomes more important than our own. We take responsibility for them, and they for us. It's really quite beautiful, don't you think?"

"Yes," Richard murmured, mesmerized by golden highlights gleaming in those rich eyes. "Beautiful."

A frantic woof broke the trance as Rags pranced happily around Lissa, who hurried down the sidewalk with her arms full of dog supplies. Her face was already flushed and sweaty.

Richard relieved his daughter of her burdens, regarded her with concern. "You look tired already, punkin. Maybe this isn't such a good idea."

Lissa jerked to a stop, clearly horrified. "Daddy! You promised."

"I know, but perhaps someplace less isolated, like a nice trip to the beach—"

"I don't wanna go to the beach," she wailed. "I

wanna go to the canyon, and swim in the trout pool, and...and... You promised!''

A familiar warmth tingled his forearm. He didn't have to look to know that C.J. had touched him. The feel of her was unique, unprecedented. He moistened his lips, would have spoken if he could have.

Fortunately, C.J. did the talking for him. ''She'll be fine, Richard. I have a cell phone.'' She patted the small, zippered pouch strapped around her waist. ''Besides, it's only ten minutes by helicopter to the nearest hospital.''

''By helicopter?'' Visions of Life Flight danced through his mind. If that tidbit of information was meant to reassure him, it failed miserably.

To her credit, C.J. bit back the smile she was fighting, gave his shoulder a stoic pat. ''Parenting is hell, ain't it, partner?'' With that and an irksome chuckle, she whistled the dog into the van, then climbed into the passenger seat and buckled her safety belt.

Lissa followed suit, clambering into the back, buckling up and hugging Rags in her lap. ''C'mon, Daddy. I can't wait to get there!''

Outnumbered, outvoted and outmaneuvered, Richard had little choice but to comply. Still, as he piloted the van away from the curb and drove toward the freeway, he couldn't suppress the niggling sensation that by day's end, life as he'd known it would never be the same.

''Don't run! You'll slip on the rocks. Stay out of the woods, the weeds will make you sick. Be careful....'' Richard flinched, balled his fists at his sides without noticing that he was being studied.

C.J.'s heart ached for him, for the terror he couldn't

control, and the courage he displayed by enduring it for the sake of his child.

Down a treed, boulder-strewn slope, the San Gabriel River meandered clear and cold, crystal-washed remnants of melting mountain snow. Lissa scampered along the rocky bank with joyous abandon while Rags dashed at her side, barking, circling, pausing to chase a fluttering butterfly or sniff a scampering lizard. It was a wondrous sight, a child and her dog romping beside a pristine river.

Too bad Richard couldn't enjoy it. C.J. scrutinized the poor guy, noting he was pale as an eggshell, and looked ready to keel over in a dead faint. She tried to refocus his attention. "Richard, will you help me unload the van?"

"In a minute," he murmured without taking his gaze from the frolicking child.

"But there's a shaded picnic table on the bluff, and I want to set our things around before someone else shows up to claim it." C.J. hoisted the small cooler to the ground, tucked the silver insulation pack under her arm. "Lissa will be fine, Richard. You don't need to stare a hole in the poor child."

"What if she falls in the river?"

"Then she'll get wet."

He was not amused. "Wet is acceptable. Drowning is not."

"In this stretch of river the water is less than three feet deep and the current is barely fast enough to float a dried leaf. As rivers go, this one is fairly benign."

"Benign or not, Lissa can't swim."

"Really?" C.J. retrieved the larger cooler, the towels and a bag of dog toys. "Then we should teach her.

There's a dammed-up swimming hole about a mile up the canyon.''

Shading his eyes, Richard moved sideways to keep Lissa in sight. ''Uh-huh.''

''Maybe after lunch.''

''Uh-huh.'' He craned his neck, moved closer to the edge. ''Watch out! Don't walk on the wet rocks, they're slippery. Be careful of those tree branches—oof!''

Air rushed from his lungs as C.J. slapped a cooler against his chest. ''Take this one now,'' she said cheerily. ''You can come back for the rest.''

If Richard had been any tighter, he'd have curled up like a twisted watch spring. As it was, his stomach felt coiled and rusty as the antiquated innards of the old clocks he refurbished as a hobby. Of course, oiling a few gears was considerably simpler than calming his own jangled nerves.

He never should have agreed to this.

''Soda?''

''Hmm? Oh, thanks.'' He accepted the icy can, twirled it between his palms while C.J. settled in the filtered shade beside him to sip from her own water bottle.

A few yards away Lissa tossed Rags's doughnut toy into the stream, then squealed encouragement as the yipping animal dived to retrieve it.

C.J. smiled. ''They're having fun, aren't they?''

''She's wearing herself out.''

''Kids have a tendency to do that.'' C.J. screwed on the bottle cap, set the water aside. ''Sometimes we have to trust them to know their own limitations.''

''Spoken like a true nonparent.'' The moment the

words left his mouth, Richard realized how pompous he sounded. He spun around just as C.J. blinked the hurt from her eyes. "I'm sorry. I had no right to say that."

She shrugged, teased him with a smile. "Well, you're right. I don't have any children, but I was one once. Doesn't that count?"

"Certainly." It was a lie, of course, and he suspected she knew that. To Richard's mind being a parent was as far removed from being a child as was, well, being a cat and a dog. Both had four legs and fur, but that's where the similarity ended.

To her credit, C.J. let the subject drop, returned her attention to the cavorting child. As soon as Rags paddled to shore and shook himself, she whistled. The dog dropped his toy and dashed over.

Lissa trudged after him, panting and looking pained. "How come you called him? We were having fun."

"Even dogs need a rest break." She poured some water into Rags's bowl, leaned against a tree while the animal lapped it up.

Richard, meanwhile, studied his daughter's flushed face with concern. She was breathing heavily, which worried him. "Are you feeling all right, punkin?"

She nodded quickly. Too quickly.

Leaning forward, C.J. pulled up her legs, hugged her knees. "Is your chest feeling tight, Lissa?"

The child shook her head violently, her eyes wide and a little desperate. A breath vibrated.

Smiling, C.J. patted a spot on the ground. "Why don't you come sit by Rags."

After a moment's hesitation, Lissa complied and, to Richard's surprise, allowed C.J. to drape an arm around her shoulders. "You know what we were discussing earlier, about taking responsibility?" The child scratched a spot of mud off her knee. "Well, we have to take responsibility for ourselves, too. Our bodies are a very precious gift. They'll take care of us, but we must take care of them, too. You give Rags what he needs, don't you? You also have to give your body what it needs, and it's not fair to your daddy or to yourself to pretend that everything is okay just because you don't want to stop playing. If you get sick, you won't be able to play for a very long time. You don't want that, do you?"

Still studying her mud-splotched knee, Lissa shook her head without looking up.

"So, is your chest feeling a little tight?" At the child's affirmative nod, C.J. squeezed her shoulders. "Maybe you'd like to keep Rags company while he takes his rest? Dogs get tired, too, you know."

With a limp shrug, Lissa patted her lap, grinning as the animal bellied over to flop across her bare legs. Her breathing seemed looser already.

Richard could hardly believe his eyes. After nearly nine years of having been wheedled, forced, coaxed and cajoled, his daughter had willingly responded to a simple request that she take responsibility for herself, a request issued not by the father who loved her, but by the woman whom until yesterday Lissa had viewed with envious fury.

What did C. J. Moray have that Richard didn't? Besides the obvious feminine attributes that he personally found exceptionally appealing. Clearly C.J. had reached his daughter on a different level, tapped a resource Richard hadn't even known existed.

Part of him was in awe; the other part was jealous as
hell. Lissa was *his* daughter, after all. He wasn't at all
certain he liked the idea that someone else might understand his own child better than he did.

C.J. shifted beside him, fumbled with the zipper of her
waist pouch. Her fingers seemed a little shaky, and when
he glanced up, he saw her face was pale, damp with
perspiration. She extracted a roll of hard candies, popped
one into her mouth, then offered the roll to Lissa, who
took one, and to Richard, who refused.

"I'm ready for lunch," she said, tucking the candy
back into the pouch. "Anyone else?"

"I'm not hungry," Lissa said, pitching a pebble into
the river. "I ate about a million pancakes for breakfast."

"And drank about a million sodas *since* breakfast."

"We've got a whole lot of sodas," Lissa argued. "We
brought bunches and bunches, and C.J. doesn't drink
soda, so I didn't want it to be wasted or anything."

"Sodas come in cans. They won't go bad if you don't
drink them all in one day." He gave one of her braids a
teasing tug. "No more sweet stuff until after lunch,
okay?"

She angled a mischievous glance. "Do I hafta spit out
my candy?"

"No, you don't have to spit out your candy, just don't
ask for any more until you've eaten something nourish-
ing."

C.J. stood, wiped her forehead and gazed up the hill
toward the picnic table strewn with their belongings.
"Speaking of nourishment and the needs of our bodies,
I'm going to grab a quick bite." She headed up the dirt

pathway, added over her shoulder, "Shall I bring anything back?"

When Lissa suggested Rags might be hungry, too, C.J. promised to return with a pocketful of doggy treats, then rounded a turn and disappeared from view.

Richard stared at the empty path without understanding why. Something bothered him, something he couldn't quite put a finger on. C.J.'s demeanor had changed. Nothing blatant, just a subtle shift from outgoing and exuberant to quietly introspective. He recalled that her fingers had trembled with the zipper on her pouch, and the happy sparkle had faded from her eyes. She'd seemed suddenly distracted, subdued.

"I'll be back in a minute," he told Lissa.

The child glanced up as he stood. "Where are you going?"

"To see if C.J. needs any help. Stay here with Rags, punkin. Don't wander off."

"Okay. Rags is still tired, anyway."

Richard smiled, felt a burst of pride as he walked the short pathway up the hill. Lissa had behaved admirably today. There'd been no tantrums, no fits of pique, no sulking or manipulation. Instead, she'd been amiable, thoughtful, a joy to be around. She was growing up, he thought, both saddened and pleased by the prospect.

As he emerged into the picnic area, a peculiar glint caught his eye, sunlight reflecting from the silver skin of the insulated pack lying open on the redwood table. C.J. stood nearby, fidgeting with something that looked like a white hand calculator. She touched her finger to a paper strip, fed the strip through a slot in the machine.

Richard stood there, stunned.

After a few seconds, C.J. glanced at the instrument's digital display, then removed the strip, tucked a sleek, penlike object into some kind of holder. By the time she'd finished replacing the equipment into the soft-sided silver pack, Richard found his voice. "You're diabetic."

C.J. glanced up, seeming neither startled by his sudden appearance nor concerned by the blunt pronouncement. "Yes. Does that bother you?"

It did, but not for the reason she thought. "You should have told me."

"Why?"

"So I'd be prepared to assist if you'd become ill." To his surprise, she burst out laughing. He strode to the table, frowning and more than a little annoyed. "I fail to see the humor in that."

She snorted, covered her mouth, snickered twice more before containing her amusement. "I'm sorry. It's just that I had this hilarious image of you trying to keep asthma medication in one pocket and insulin in the other, then getting the pockets confused in a crisis. You'd probably shove the inhaler down my throat and put poor Lissa into a coma."

He scraped her with a look. "This may come as a shock to you, but I'm not really a bumbling imbecile." A twitch at the corner of his mouth gave away the smile he'd been fighting. "I only play one on TV."

Laughing openly, she zipped the insulated pack, tossed it aside and turned her attention to her plastic lunch container. "I didn't mean to make fun of you."

"Yes, you did."

"Okay, I did." She popped the plastic lid, retrieved a

smaller container filled with what appeared to be potato salad. "But I only make fun of people I like."

"Then you must like me a lot."

Something flickered through her eyes a moment before she looked away. "Yes," she said softly. "I do."

A peculiar warmth slipped down his spine. Every trace of moisture evaporated from his mouth. She liked him. A lot. He suddenly felt like a teenager favored by a smile from the most popular girl in class.

Avoiding his gaze, C.J. sat on the bench, used a plastic fork to spear a potato chunk. "Would you like some? It's made with fat-free mayo."

"No, thanks—" Horrified by the adolescent squeak of his voice, he coughed, shifted, squared his shoulders. "No, thank you."

She shrugged, angled a wary glance. "You'll excuse me if I go ahead? Growing girls need their carbos."

"Carbos?"

"Carbohydrates."

He shook his head, tried not to ogle her lean, bare thighs. She must be at least five feet eight inches, he thought, and was startled he hadn't realized before how stately she was. And how incredibly lovely. His body tightened appreciatively.

"Sure you don't want some?"

"Huh?" Richard was horrified that she'd read his wayward thoughts, and his gaze snapped from her luscious thighs to the forked potato chunk she was offering him. "Oh. No. Thank you." Relieved, he cleared his throat, forced himself to avoid eye contact. "Please, enjoy your lunch."

She smiled, nodded, chewed.

He shuffled a moment, then settled beside her. "You require regular meals, don't you?"

"Doesn't everybody?"

"Well, everybody has to eat, of course. I only meant that in your case, er, that is, in your delicate condition—"

Her gleeful hoot startled him. "My *what?* Good grief, Richard, I'm diabetic, not pregnant."

If the sudden burning of his cheeks was any clue, he must be glowing like a neon tomato. "I don't suppose there's any graceful way for me to extricate myself from this, is there?"

"Graceful? Nah." She forked up another bite of salad, chewed thoughtfully. "But don't stop on my account. Actually, I'm enjoying this immensely."

"Quite the little sadist, aren't you?"

"Bobbi thinks so."

Richard's heart gave a disappointed thunk. "Your boyfriend?"

"Hmm?" A perplexed frown crinkled, disappeared with the hike of her brows. "Who, Bobbi?" She chuckled. "Hardly. She's my roommate."

There was no reason on earth he should be so relieved by that news. "Roommate. Of course, the one who let Rags get away."

"The very same." She brushed her hands together, retrieved a bag of cold cuts from her lunch container. "Turkey?"

He helped himself to a slice. "Where were you, by the way?"

"Where was I when?"

"The day Rags got lost."

"Oh." She popped the paper-thin slice into her mouth,

chewed without rushing and washed it down with a sip of bottled water.

Richard presumed she was considering whether or not to answer his question.

It took a moment, but she finally did answer. "I was in the hospital." That didn't shock him, but he was unduly upset by the image of this vibrant, athletic woman felled by illness. She washed down another bite, then continued matter-of-factly. "Bobbi, Rags and I had planned to spend a day at her parents' mountain cabin. A snowstorm rolled in, kept us pinned down for two days. There wasn't any heat in the cabin, and although extreme cold doesn't normally affect insulin stability, it can affect the body's ability to assimilate it. And of course, we hadn't brought enough food, either. To make a long story short, I had a bad reaction."

"And ended up in the hospital."

She shrugged. "It happens."

"Which proves my point."

"What point is that?"

"You should have told me."

Her smile was indulgent, not unkind. "My physical well-being is not your responsibility," she said, clearing away the remnants of her lunch. "Besides, I wear a Medic Alert tag on a neckchain. If an unforeseen crisis should occur, I imagine some clever paramedic would eventually notice it and get a clue."

"You're making fun of me again."

"No, your concern is admirable, just unwarranted." She snapped the plastic container top. "I'm wearing a swimsuit under my clothes in case anyone was in the mood to get wet. Are you?"

The image of C. J. Moray's lithe, bikini-clad body flashed through his mind. "Oh, yeah," he murmured with a sly smile. "I am definitely in the mood."

The trail to the swimming hole followed the meandering river through a pine forest, where the waterway narrowed with small rapids, then blossomed into a deep green pool created by a man-made rock dam. Lissa and Rags led the way. Rags took point, barking encouragement to the lagging humans as he dashed several yards down the pathway, then scurried back to hurry them along.

Richard positioned himself at the rear of the tiny column, right behind C.J., who sauntered casually, pausing frequently to scoop up a smooth, weatherworn rock, or test the texture of a puzzle-bark pine with her fingertip. Everything delighted her, from dappled shadows dancing across the water to the lustrous polish of egg-shaped granite ground smooth as glass in the tumbling belly of the stream.

She was holding such a stone now, caressing it between her palms. The gesture was gentle, natural, incredibly erotic. She worshiped the smooth, round stone, turning it in her hand, squeezing ever so softly while her thumb provocatively stroked the polished surface.

Richard broke out in a cold sweat.

"Isn't it incredible?" Her voice was a husky whisper, as if she feared disturbing the tranquillity of this mystical place. "Look how it gleams in the sunlight, all sparkling and glittery. It's beautiful, isn't it?"

"Uh-huh." Richard felt his Adam's apple bounce and wedge in his throat as she rubbed the stone against her cheek, purring in ecstasy. Her eyes fluttered shut, a serene smile touched her lips. She looked for all the world like a satisfied woman nuzzling a cherished lover.

When she heaved a contented sigh, Richard swallowed a groan. Sweat dripped into his eyes. A muscle in his groin twitched. He shifted, coughed, tried to yank his gaze from her beautiful, passion-sated face. "Er, perhaps we should, ah, continue."

"I suppose," she murmured, still nuzzling her cheek against the smooth stone. Inhaling deeply, she opened her eyes, smiled and held out the rock. "Do you want to hold it?"

Considering the images still flickering through his naughty mind, he most certainly did not want to hold it, and said so.

"Would you put it in your pocket for me?"

"I beg your pardon?"

"Your pocket," she repeated. "I want to take this rock home."

"Oh."

At the moment, his pocket was being crowded from within, but he forced a thin smile, nodded and managed not to flinch when she snatched his hand and reverently placed her treasure in his stiff palm. As soon as she'd turned away, he shifted himself, jammed the stupid rock in the pocket and cringed at the pressure.

Testosterone overload was not what he had expected from a casual canyon nature hike.

Of course, nothing had gone as expected from the day C. J. Moray had swirled into his life. That had been less than a week ago. It felt like a lifetime. Everything seemed changed somehow. Lissa was different. Certainly Richard was different. Even life itself seemed different.

Expecting the unexpected was, well, exhilarating, particularly for a cautious-by-nature architect who hadn't experienced true excitement since the night his college baseball team won the league playoffs.

"Daddy, look! A real log bridge!"

With some effort Richard tore his gaze from the golden-haired goddess in front of him long enough to focus on his squealing daughter, who was pointing to a rotten tree trunk spanning the deepest part of the swimming hole. "Don't cross it," he warned. "It doesn't look safe."

Before the words were out of his mouth, Rags scampered to the middle of the log, then stood there barking proudly.

C.J. laughed, ducked beneath a tree limb extending across the narrow path. "There are only two ways to reach the beach on the other side," she said, nodding toward a gently sloped expanse of washed pebbles extending into the pool. "Rags is showing you the dry route." As she spoke, she turned sideways, pressing her back against the eroded bank that jutted like a small cliff on one side while the expanding pool lapped at the edge of the shrinking path. "For obvious reasons, we can't stay here."

Richard silently agreed, and would have done so aloud except that C.J. reached out to balance herself with a twig growing out of the rocky soil. From the corner of his eye he saw the twig rear back, fork a twitchy tongue. C.J. saw it, too.

That's when all hell broke loose.

Chapter Four

"*S*nake!"

C.J.'s frantic screech bounced off canyon walls like a death knell. "Snake, snake—" she spun on the skinny path, grabbed Richard's shirt collar and shook frantically "—snake, snake, snake, snake, *sna-ake!*"

His eyes popped wide open, his head whipped wildly around. "Where? *Where?*" Clearly horrified, he stumbled back a step, whirled as if preparing to sprint away.

"Oh, no, you don't!" C.J. hooked a forearm around his throat, spun him like a top. "You're not leaving me here. Kill it!" She wiggled a frantic finger at the reptile just as it slithered onto the path, eighteen horrifying inches of black-and-gray-striped terror that was every bit as thick as the average pencil.

C.J. shrieked loud enough to pop a larynx, planted a foot on Richard's hipbone and climbed him like a fence. *"Kill it!"*

Gagging, half-smothered, Richard stumbled back, one

arm flapping for balance, the other clawing her shirt. "Get off," he sputtered. "Can't see."

Intellectually, C.J. was quite aware of his vision impairment, since her head-hugging frenzy was squashing his face into her midsection. But intellect had nothing to do with her raw terror at the sight of the reptile's glossy black eyes and shuddery slithering body.

She cast a horrified glance over her shoulder. "It's coming!" She shrieked, heaved a leg over his shoulder. "It's right by your foot! We're going to die!"

Lurching backward, Richard kicked out a leg for balance, made peculiar little gagging sounds as C.J. chin-choked him to straddle his shoulder, digging one heel into the small of his back and the other into his stomach. She shrieked, grabbed his ears and nearly twisted his head off when the snake reared up, twitching its ugly forked tongue.

Richard clawed at her arms, managed to peer beneath her elbow long enough to get a glimpse of the beast. "Arghhhh!" He let out a second bellow, then a third and whipped around so fast that C.J. didn't have time to duck. As he sprinted down the path, a drooping branch snagged her chin. Richard would have kept right on running if C.J. hadn't maintained a death grip on his skull. One minute she was riding him up the path spurring his ribs with her heels, the next they were both spinning in place.

Richard gurgled, bounced off the jutting bank and lurched forward, arms rotating madly. C.J. screamed, straightened, grabbed a fistful of his hair and tried to rein him in. It was too late. He pitched forward, and they both plummeted into the icy pool.

Flailing frantically, C.J. sank into the frigid water.

Bubbles murmured past her ears. Her feet touched rock. She bent her knees, pushed and rocketed to the surface, sputtering.

Richard's head popped up a moment later. He was coughing, his face red as a boiled beet. "Are you—" he paused to gasp "—crazy?"

"Me?" She shook water out of her eyes, kicking madly beneath the surface to keep from sinking again. "You're the one who jumped into the stupid river."

"Like I had a choice? There was a madwoman on my head."

"I wouldn't have been on your head if you'd done the manly thing, and killed the damned snake."

"I hate snakes," he hissed. "At the moment, I'm not too fond of you, either."

"Coward."

"Lunatic."

"Snake-hating sissy." A smile threatened.

His eyes gleamed. "Man-climbing maniac."

She chuckled, swished around in the pool in time to see Rags dart across the log bridge, barking wildly. The animal dashed up the path, skidded to a stop right in front of the coiled reptile. "Rags, no!"

The dog whined, sniffed the snake, which wiggled a thready tongue before swishing around and slinking back into the underbrush. Rags issued an all-clear woof, then pranced proudly back to meet Lissa, who crouched on the log with enormous eyes. "It was just a little gard'ner snake, Daddy. Danny D'Angelo brought one just like it for show-and-tell. Teacher gave him a gold star." As an afterthought she added, "Are you okay, Daddy?"

Richard shoved a wet tangle of hair from his face,

angled a sheepish glance at his worried daughter. "I'm fine, punkin." As if to prove the point, he stroked smoothly toward the pebbled beach, shoulder muscles rippling, sneakered feet kicking up a froth close enough to submerge C.J. in a small tidal wave.

She bobbed back to the surface, sputtering, would have issued a strenuous protest had her left calf muscle not twisted itself into a sudden knot of searing agony. Her grunt of pain drowned in a burst of bubbles as she coiled to grab her leg, and sank to the bottom of the pool.

Engulfed by a watery roar, she twisted, kicked, tried to press the knotted muscle for relief. Nothing worked.

Her lungs tightened, ached, burned. Her leg was useless, grotesquely bent by the spasm. Unable to kick, she tried to use cupped hands to pull herself toward the surface, but the awkward twist of her leg sent her spiraling out of control.

At least, she thought she was out of control. Maybe not. Maybe down was up and up was down. Who could say? Certainly not C.J., whose oxygen-starved brain was desperate to the point of hallucination, and her lungs felt ready to burst.

She blinked, saw a curious trout watching her, and giggled out the remainder of precious oxygen. She wanted to pet the fish. If only her leg didn't hurt so much—

Something snagged the back of her collar, rocketing her upward. She broke the surface gasping, wheezing, sucking air into her lungs so fast it was a wonder she didn't float skyward like a blimp.

Vaguely aware she was being pulled through the water, C.J. was limp, disoriented. She heard a soothing voice, felt cobbles against her back, realized she was lying on the pebble beach.

A warm arm slipped under her shoulders, turned her. She coughed, spit water. Distant barking seemed closer now, more clear. A frantic tongue swished her ear.

"Why, Richard," she murmured. "I didn't know you cared."

A masculine chuckle enveloped her like a cashmere blanket. "So you like having your ear licked, hmm? I'll remember that."

She blinked, turned her face and was rewarded by a sloppy canine kiss. "Rags?"

Richard's laugh was rich, deep, delicious. "You sound disappointed."

The dizziness easing, C.J. flopped back on the beach, grinned up at the man bending over her. He was quite handsome, actually, not nearly as average as she'd first thought. Maybe it was the soggy raft of hair plastered across his forehead that gave him a rakish appeal. Maybe it was the way his pecs vibrated beneath a soaking-wet T-shirt that left little to the imagination. Maybe it was the fact that he'd just saved her life. Whatever it was, something had definitely changed. C.J. would never view him as average again.

"Yes, I'm disappointed," she murmured, flinching as her calf muscle spasmed sharply. "Here I thought I'd found a genuine, dyed-in-the-wool ear nuzzler." She flinched again, bit her lip and struggled to sit up while reaching for her leg.

Richard beat her to it. "Muscle cramp?" When she nodded, he knelt to inspect it, lightly fingered the bulging knot. "This might hurt a bit."

C.J. howled as his fingertips pressed into the twisted muscle. "Are you trying to kill me?"

"Not at the moment." Using the flat of his hand, he massaged her calf, grinning as she spouted colorful epithets and dire threats to his manhood. "Now, now, there are pets and small children nearby."

"I apologize to the child," C.J. said through her teeth. "But Rags has heard it before.... Ouch, ouch, *ouch!*" Despite her protests, the pain was easing. His hands were so warm. So strong. So efficient. "Ouch," she added lamely, lest he realize how much she was enjoying his attention. She closed her eyes as his palms glided across her tingling flesh. She heaved a happy sigh. "Ouch."

Life was good. A sense of well-being rolled over her, melting her insides like warm pudding. Sunlight dried her skin, heated her blood. The soft lap of water on rock soothed her as Richard's strong hands expertly kneaded her flesh.

Only his hands weren't exactly kneading anymore. Purposeful medicinal massage had been replaced by something softer, gentler. More erotic.

With some effort she opened one eye. The breath backed up in her throat. His eyes were dark, glowing, his lips loose, nostrils slightly flared like a studhorse on scent. He was in serious lust.

Even worse, so was she.

The tingling sensation in her calf had marched steadily upward until her thighs were on fire, and her belly ached with unrequited need.

He spoke—whispered, actually—in a throaty rasp that gave her goose bumps. "I nuzzle ears, too."

The mere suggestion made her giddy with excitement. "A man of many talents."

"Many, many talents."

Heather smoke wafted from his gaze, and C.J. was struck completely mute. She could only imagine the talents to which he referred. And she had an excellent imagination. Her upper lip beaded moisture even as her throat went dry. She was just about to grab him by the throat screaming, "Take me, big boy," when his gaze settled somewhere beyond her, and his eyes widened.

From his squatting position he lurched backward as if to sit on his heels, missed and fell over, then scrambled sideways like a frantic crab. He seemed to be saying something, but all C.J. could make out was a series of garbled grunts, drowned out by a childish voice disturbingly close to her own reclining head.

"I want a gold star, too."

A cold spear of terror stabbed straight through her spine. She spun on the pebbled ground, came face to glossy-eyed face with the tongue-flicking snake wound around Lissa's hand.

C.J.'s body froze, but her frantic brain analyzed options at lightning speed. Screaming was one course of action. Running wildly was another. Behind her, Richard leapt up to pursue both options at once, so C.J. did likewise.

Rags barked. Lissa pleaded. The snake wriggled. All hell broke loose again.

It had been that kind of day.

"The bleeding has almost stopped," C.J. said, amused by Richard's sour expression. "Next time you're trying to break the world speed record for swim-sprinting, duck under the log bridge.''

He threw a withering glance over his shoulder. "I'll keep that in mind.''

She shifted a smile. "I still think you need a couple stitches.''

He yanked a cooler out of the van, set it on the sidewalk in front. "What I need is a stiff drink.''

"I wish I could join you." C.J. took the insulated pack he handed her, along with her own small cooler. "I wouldn't mind a stiff mineral water with lime, though.''

He grunted, handed a bag of doggy supplies to Lissa, who'd sulked most of the way home.

"It was only a little gard'ner snake," she muttered.

"Garter, not gardener.''

"Whatever." She kicked the grass. "I coulda had a gold star.''

"You could have had a snakebite, too.''

"Gart-ner snakes can't hurt you. Teacher said so.''

"With all due respect to your teacher, snakes are snakes." Richard handed the Frisbee to Rags, who took the beloved item in his mouth and trotted toward the front porch. "I've told you never, ever to touch them. They're slimy and—''

"Uh-uh! They feel real smooth and silky, kind of like the polished handrail on the stairs at Gramps's house.''

Richard quelled her with a look. "I don't care what they feel like, you are never to go near one again. They slither, they squeeze and they bite.''

C.J. grimaced at the apt description. "Your daddy is right, Lissa. Snakes are, well, snakes." She shuddered, hauled the unloaded picnic items over to her own car and tossed them in the trunk.

Lissa followed, pleading her case. "But Charlie wouldn't hurt anybody. He was just a baby."

"Charlie?" C.J. smiled at the girl's solemn nod. "Well, if, er, Charlie was really that young it would have been cruel to take him away from his mommy."

"Charlie doesn't need a mommy."

"Everyone needs a mommy."

The child's brows puckered. "I don't."

A determined quiver in the child's voice broke C.J.'s heart. She slammed the trunk, spun around, horrified by her faux pas. Although C.J. didn't know the details, Richard had mentioned that Lissa's mother had died years ago, and she could have kicked herself for being so insensitive. "Oh, sweetie. I'm sorry. I forgot—" She cut herself off, hugged the girl instead. "But you are blessed with a very special daddy," she murmured against the girl's pigtailed scalp. "If Charlie has a wonderful daddy like you do, don't you think he'd be very sad to be taken away from him?"

Lissa sniffed, stepped back, considered that for a moment. "Yeah, I guess so. I mean, I'd be real lonesome without Daddy." Rags dashed up, panting, to run circles around Lissa's legs. The child giggled, shifted the bag in her hand to pet the shaggy, bouncing head. "Anyway, I've still got Ragsy."

The familiar lump of loss wedged in C.J.'s throat, but not as painfully as before. "Yes," she whispered. "You've still got Rags."

Smiling, she watched dog and girl scurry toward the house, barking and laughing respectively, with a sense of comfort that their friendship filled a special need for each of them.

A tingling warmth alerted her to Richard's presence. She glanced over her shoulder, felt her heart lurch at his nearness.

"I don't know how you do it," he murmured, gazing at his frolicking daughter. "You've turned a sulky, miserable child into a happy, delightful little girl."

"Children are usually happy when they're having fun, and miserable when they're not. It's a fact of nature, I suppose."

"I suppose." He regarded her in a manner more introspective than scrutinizing. After a moment, a decisive glint touched his gaze. "How about that mineral water? I squeeze a mean lime." Apparently reading C.J.'s surprise as reluctance, he angled a glance across the yard, assuring himself that his daughter was out of hearing range before offering a silky smile that melted resistance as effectively as sunlight on a snow cone. "Lissa will be going to bed in a couple of hours."

The implication gave her goose bumps. "You've got a deal."

Grinning, Richard hiked a bruised and bandaged brow, flexed his manly biceps as he hoisted the cooler, then grasped her elbow with his free hand and ushered her up the sidewalk toward the house. Lissa dashed across the yard, sprinted in front of them with Rags on her heels, twisted the knob and dashed inside.

Richard skidded to a stop, his jaw drooping.

C.J. frowned. "Do you always leave your front door unlocked?"

"No." He spit out the word like a bad taste, strode up the steps muttering to himself.

C.J. followed anxiously, emerged into a homey living room that seemed perfectly normal except for dozens and dozens of unique clocks settled in every nook and cranny. The room was cluttered, but showed no signs of having been ransacked. Unless one counted the tangled tools and gutted clock parts strewn across the dining table.

A sigh of relief turned into a gasp as a familiar male voice boomed from the kitchen. "It's about time you two got home. Mother's been holding supper for almost an hour."

C.J. stiffened. Richard moaned. Rags whined and slunk under the coffee table.

Only Lissa was pleased by the unexpected turn of events. "Gramps!" she chortled, dashing toward the kitchen just as the big man emerged. "We had a picnic, and went for a hike, and Charlie scared Daddy and C.J. so bad they jumped in the river with all their clothes on, and Daddy bumped his head on a log, so we didn't get to go swimming 'cause Daddy was all wet anyway, and besides he was bleeding so we had to come home, but we had a really, really good time, and it was more fun than I ever had in my whole entire life!"

Thompson McCade stared over his granddaughter's head with a look cold enough to freeze meat. "What's that woman doing here?"

Richard lowered the cooler to the floor. A muscle twitched in his jaw. "Ms. Moray is my guest," he said quietly. "A more appropriate question might be what are you doing here?"

"This is my daughter's house," he snapped, as if that

answered the question. He turned his icy gaze on C.J., although he clearly wasn't speaking to her. "We assumed you'd be hungry after your outing. Mother wanted to fix you a nice meal, and this is the thanks she gets?"

C.J. stepped sideways, gazed past the furious man to see his obviously unhappy wife in the kitchen, wringing her hands in the same way she'd done the day C.J. had first met her.

Richard raked his hair, flinched as his fingers brushed his lacerated forehead. "I wish you'd let me know what you planned. We've already eaten."

"We went to Burger House," Lissa added, oblivious to the tension between the two men she loved most in the world. "C.J. has to eat all the time, 'cause she's got diet-beaters."

Thompson blinked. "You mean diabetes?"

Lissa nodded happily. "She's got a really cool machine that reads glue levels and everything!"

"Er, glucose levels." C.J.'s smile stiffened into a cringe at Thompson's thunderous expression. "I'm terribly sorry you and your wife were inconvenienced. If we'd known you were waiting for us—"

"We were not waiting for you, young woman. We were waiting for our family."

Even Lissa stumbled back at his sharp tone. Richard was visibly livid. "Lissa, I think C.J. would enjoy seeing your puppet collection."

"I really should get going…" The words died on C.J.'s lips at Richard's silent plea. "Just as soon as Lissa shows me her puppets," she finished lamely.

"Yay!" Lissa clapped happily. "My puppets are really, really cool. Last summer Gramps and Gramma went to Germany, and they brought back a real, live Pinocchio! Well, not alive live, but almost!''

She grabbed C.J.'s hand and steered her past a towering steeple clock, around a shelf of ticking mantel pieces, into a hallway decorated with ticking wall units of every type and description, and finally into a beautiful chintz bedroom with shelves and shelves of colorful, painted puppets.

It seemed a fitting collection for such a lonely child, an entire roomful of friends with whom she could share her isolated life.

Each puppet was lovingly retrieved for inspection, and C.J. was properly impressed, admiring every one for its uniqueness and its beauty. Throughout the process, Lissa beamed proudly, clearly enthralled by sharing her special things, and either unaware of or unmoved by the rumble of angry male voices filtering from beyond the hallway.

C.J. was neither unaware nor unmoved. There was an unhealthy undercurrent rippling between the people Lissa loved most, something secretive, something fearful.

The logical course of action would be for C.J. to withdraw from a situation over which she had no control, and which clearly did not concern her. Then again, she'd never been one to let logic get in the way of helping people she cared about.

And yes, C.J. was willing to admit she cared about Richard and Lissa. She just wasn't willing to admit how much.

If not for Lissa's constant chatter, the dinner table would have been silent as a morgue. C.J., who again asked herself why on earth she'd agreed to share a meal she did not want, forked a piece of pot roast to the side of her plate and buried it beneath a mound of untouched mashed potatoes.

Actually, C.J. knew exactly why she'd stayed. Richard had asked her to. One look into those soft, pleading eyes and she'd been helpless to resist.

"...So after Daddy and C.J. finally got out of the pool, Ragsy and I went looking for Charlie." Lissa paused to shovel in another bite of potatoes, swallowed quickly lest a lag dilute the power of her story. "Ragsy found him under a bush, and Charlie just wiggled right into my hand. I wanted to bring him home so bad, but Daddy got all freaked and swam into the log and his head was all bleeding so C.J. had to put a 'fly bandage on it—"

"Butterfly bandage," Richard corrected, reaching out to dab his daughter's milky mouth with a napkin. "And such details really aren't appropriate for dinner conversation."

"Let the child talk." Across the table, Thompson McCade set down his wineglass, oblivious to Richard's pained expression or the quiet reproach of his own stoic wife. "You should have allowed Lissa to keep her snake, Richard. I certainly would have."

Poor Sarah McCade nearly choked on her food. She covered her mouth with her napkin, stared over the cloth with huge, horrified eyes.

Richard simply laid down his fork, steepled his hands. "There will be no reptiles in this house. End of discussion."

"Ah, yes. I'd forgotten that dreadful fear you have of such creatures." McCade made no attempt to disguise his contempt. "Fortunately for my granddaughter, at least

one of the men in her life has a modicum of courage."
He turned to Lissa with a patronizing smile. "Never fear,
precious girl. Gramps will buy you the biggest, wriggliest
snake we can find, and you may keep it at my house out
of respect for—" a derisive snort "—your father's irrational terror."

The reaction around the table was simultaneous and
expectedly diverse.

"Now, see here, McCade—"

"Oh, Thompson, dear, do you really think that's a
good idea?"

"Really, Gramps? Ooo, that's so cool!"

C.J. snatched up the nearest bowl. "More potatoes,
anyone?"

Richard threw down his napkin, stood so quickly the
chair legs rasped the roughened tile. "I said *no snakes.*"

"But, Daddy—"

"*No!*"

Lissa hopped up, sobbing, and dashed out of the room.
Richard skewered McCade with a black look, then followed his daughter.

Sarah murmured, "Oh, dear."

McCade turned on C.J. "Now see what you've done."

C.J. glanced around, touched her own sternum. "Me?"

"Of course 'you.'" McCade finished his wine,
slammed the empty glass back on the table. "You've
caused nothing but trouble since the moment you showed
up. If you had the slightest trace of a conscience, you'd
go back to wherever it is you came from and never
darken this family's door again." A low growl caught
McCade's attention. He glared down as Rags bared his
teeth. "And take that mangy mutt with you."

Sarah touched her husband's arm. "Now, dear, Lissa is very fond of that little dog. She'd be very sad without him." McCade grumbled, shifted in his chair. "Besides, I think you're being rather unfair to Ms. Moray. She's only trying to help."

"Help?" McCade stared at his wife in disbelief. "By trying to destroy an entire family?"

C.J. found her voice. "I beg your pardon, Mr. McCade, but I hardly see the connection between suggesting a nature hike and human destruction."

"I wouldn't expect a woman like you to understand," he muttered, retrieving a wallet from the inside pocket of his tailored sport coat.

"A woman like *me?* What the heck is that supposed—?"

McCade whipped out a photograph of a lovely brunette with wary eyes and a timid smile.

C.J.'s shoulders loosened, and a fine ache touched her chest. "She's beautiful."

"Yes," McCade whispered, while his wife gazed into space with red eyes. "She was very beautiful, and very young." The man stiffened, replaced the picture in his wallet. "She's dead, you know."

Sarah flinched but said nothing.

"I know," C.J. replied. "I'm sorry."

Tucking his wallet back into his coat, McCade focused piercing blue eyes that made C.J. shiver. "She's dead, but she's not gone. She will always be my daughter, just as she will always be Lissa's mother—" A frisson of anxiety skittered down C.J.'s spine as she realized what was coming next. "And she will always be Richard's wife."

C.J. sat quietly, neither blinking nor refuting that.

McCade leaned forward, eyes cold as winter glass. "No one will ever take my daughter's place."

C.J.'s gaze didn't waver. "Of course not."

For several long seconds the visual stalemate remained unbroken. Finally McCade pushed away from the table and stood. "As long as we understand each other."

No reply was given and none was expected. Only a fool would ignore so blatant a warning, and C. J. Moray had never considered herself a fool.

Until now.

Chapter Five

"Yikes, bummer." Bobbi flopped onto the sofa, kicked up her stockinged feet and nibbled the corner of a homemade, macadamia-chocolate-chip cookie so tempting C.J. would have killed for a single bite. Bobbi chewed, swallowed, washed it down with a sloppy gulp of milk. "The old man sounds like a bad-tempered bear with a thorn in his paw. What did you do?"

C.J. shrugged, settled in the lounge chair with her plate of fresh fruit. "What could I do? I helped Lissa's grandmother clean up the kitchen, then I left."

"Just like that?"

"Just like that."

"Gee, Ceejz, it's not like you to let some pompous old geezer shove you around that way. Why didn't you tell him off?"

A good question, C.J. decided, and one she'd been asking herself all evening. As it was, she'd nearly bitten her tongue off to keep from suggesting Thompson

McCade store his smelly old pipe in an innovative and painfully personal locale. "It would have just made matters worse, Bobbi. Besides, I felt sorry for Sarah McCade. All the poor woman wants is peace in her own family. Or at least, what's left of her family."

Bobbi set down her milk glass, wiped her mouth with her sleeve. "It must be tough losing a daughter. If anything happened to me, my mom would be upset for, oh, at least a couple of days."

"Bobbi!" C.J. sighed, put off by but not unused to her roommate's black humor. "Just because you and your mother don't get along doesn't mean that she doesn't love you."

"I know." A flash of pain, a sober stare. "Don't mind me. Mother's Day always makes me a little goofy."

"That was weeks ago."

Bobbi shrugged. "I hold a grudge."

"You still haven't heard from her?"

"Nah." She snagged another cookie, took an angry bite. "I didn't expect to. For all I know, she didn't even get the flowers I sent. Maybe the maid just stuck them in water while Ma was gallivanting around Europe. I never know where she is."

Since C.J. couldn't think of anything soothing to say, she simply nibbled her fruit in silence. It was sadly unfair, she thought, that mothers and daughters were so frequently mismatched. C.J.'s own mother had loved her children dearly, yet used them as weapons in her marital war of martyrdom. Bobbi's mother, who'd never wanted the bother or responsibility of children despite having brought three of them into the world, considered offspring unwanted obstacles to her freedom. In contrast,

Sarah McCade, whose life clearly revolved around love for her family, had been left childless and grieving by senseless tragedy.

"What happened to her?" Bobbi asked suddenly.

"To who, Richard's wife?" When her friend nodded, C.J. replied with a shrug. "I don't know. He told me she died when Lissa was quite young, but didn't go into specifics."

"And you didn't ask?"

"It wasn't any of my business."

"Of course it's your business, girl! How in hell are you going to snag yourself a husband if you don't find out all there is to know about his past relationships?"

C.J. nearly choked on a bite of apple. She coughed, sputtered, set the half-eaten fruit aside and stared in disbelief. "Have you lost your ever-loving mind? I don't want a husband."

"Sure you do. You're just too stubborn to admit it."

"I am *not* stubborn." She folded her arms, glared across the room while Bobbi snickered. "All right, maybe a little stubborn, but one thing has nothing to do with another."

"So now you're saying that you don't ever want to get married?"

She squirmed, noticed a juice spot on the hem of her shirt and worried it with a fingernail. "Never is a long time, I suppose. Maybe someday, but not now. I have my work, my friends, my freedom. Everything in my life is exactly the way I like it."

"You wouldn't change anything?" Bobbi teased. "Not one itsy-bitsy thing?"

"Well, maybe one thing."

"I knew it," Bobbi hooted. She swung her legs around, leaned forward with her chin in her hands. "You want a man in your life, right?"

"Wrong. I want a woman out of my life."

Bobbi's chin slipped off her hands. "Me? You want to get rid of *me?* Why?"

"For one thing, the bathroom mirror is always smeared with toothpaste."

"Hey, can I help it if brushing my teeth makes me sneeze? Besides, I wipe it off."

"Yes, with *my* bath towel."

"Yours is cleaner than mine."

"That's because your towel is always wadded on the floor. You never make your bed, either."

"Why bother? I'm just going to mess it up again in a few hours. Tell you what, I'll keep my bedroom door closed, then you won't have to look at it." Her anxiety tugged at C.J.'s heart. "What else? I'll change, honest. I won't even tape newspaper over the windows and stain the kitchen sink with darkroom chemicals, only don't kick me out, Ceejz, please? Then I'd have to move in with Maury, who's so damned old-fashioned he'd probably make me marry him first."

C.J. grinned. "Uh-huh."

"You sneaky goose," Bobbi growled. "You don't want to get rid of me, you want to marry me off."

"Maury loves you, hon, and he's a good man."

"I don't want to get married."

"Sure, you do. You're just scared you'll end up like your mother."

"Yeah? Well, right back atcha, babe." Bobbi's puckered frown couldn't disguise the sparkle in her eye. "We're two of a kind, aren't we?"

C.J. leaned back with an indulgent smile. "Yes, I suppose we are. Except for the toothpaste thing—"

"Again with the toothpaste? Sheesh, what a nag." Heaving a telling sigh, Bobbi grabbed another gooey cookie, settled back with a reflective expression. "You know," she said between bites, "I guess we're both destined for spinsterhood, a boring life without romance."

"Life without romance? Egads. Kill me now." C.J. laughed, pushed the dull fruit plate away. "Marriage and romance are two entirely different animals. The former is not for me, but I have no intention whatsoever of giving up the latter."

"You are a wicked woman, Ceejz."

C.J. smiled. "Well, maybe a little." Her smile wavered as her cruel and calculating roommate took another bite of cookie, then moaned in ecstasy.

"Umm-m." Bobbi licked sweet chocolate off her fingertips. "Yummy-yum-yum. Delicious, better than sex."

C.J. pitched a grape at her. "I really hate you."

Bobbi grinned. "I know."

McCade laid his pipe in the ashtray, leaned forward with his elbows on his knees. "You can't be serious."

"I'm not going to argue the point with you, Thompson. Either you treat my guests with courtesy and respect, or you won't be welcome in my home."

A red vein throbbed in the older man's temple. "This is my daughter's house—"

"Not anymore," Richard snapped, then balled his fist on the chair arm as Sarah McCade flinched in pain. He took a deep breath, softened his tone. "Melinda is gone. I wish she wasn't, but she is, and turning on each other won't change that. Lissa and I have to get on with our lives."

McCade vibrated as if struck. "It's that woman, isn't it? You want her."

A slow heat crawled up Richard's throat, concealed, he hoped, by the dull living-room lamplight. "C.J. is good for Lissa."

"Good for Lissa, or good for you?" There was no mistaking the cold fury in McCade's eyes, or the implication of words spit out like bitter poison.

"Yes, C.J. is good for me, too. She has a way of putting things into perspective, dismissing what doesn't matter and concentrating on what does. I need that. So does Lissa."

"Lissa needs her mother." McCade's voice was low, deadly. "Thanks to you, she doesn't have that anymore."

As usual, the accusation was thrown like a gut punch. Air rushed out of Richard's lungs, as it always did. And Sarah McCade, bless her, spoke up, just as both men had known she would to keep the argument from escalating. "Thompson, please. That's cruel and unfair."

McCade snatched his cold pipe from the ashtray, tucked it in his coat pocket as he stood. "Let's go, Mother."

Sarah rose nervously, angled a haunted glance at the son-in-law she'd always treated with kindness and respect, then followed her furious husband out of the house.

Richard closed the front door behind them, blew out a breath. A wave of nausea passed quietly, as it always did after contentious confrontation. Such unpleasant scenes were thankfully rare. Richard was usually an agreeable, amiable sort. Too agreeable. Too amiable. In retrospect, perhaps that had been his downfall. And his wife's.

Turning from the door, he reached for the lamp switch. His hand hovered, moved toward a framed photograph beside the antique brass parlor clock Melinda had bought him on their honeymoon. The picture, too, was from their honeymoon, one of their few happy moments together.

There had been secrets in their marriage, dark secrets that had ruined their intimacy, ravaged their family. If his wife had trusted him enough to reveal those secrets, she might still be alive. But she hadn't trusted him, hadn't trusted anyone, and Richard had been too consumed by his own obsession with building a career to notice his own wife's descent into oblivion.

So in a very real sense, Thompson McCade was right. Richard's blind ambition had destroyed a daughter, a mother, a wife. The guilt would haunt him forever.

He held the peculiar booted objects up, squinting with blatant disdain. "They look like ice skates with wheels. Tell me again why we're doing this?"

"It's good exercise." C.J. sat on the van's back bumper, enjoying Richard's reluctance as she strapped on her own rollerblades. "And it's fun."

"'Fun' is a subjective term," he grumbled. "What's wrong with walking?"

"Oh, Daddy, that's boring." A helmeted Lissa rolled cautiously out from behind the van, stiff arms held out for balance. Awkward but enthusiastic, the child practiced the toe stops C.J. had taught her, then yanked up a drooping elbow pad and adjusted her knee guards. "Besides, C.J. says rollerblading is, like, the hippest, a really cool thing to do. Don't you wanna be cool, Daddy?''

"Not particularly."

C.J. snickered, tucked her hair under her helmet. "I would have rented you the 'slow-roll starter' model, except they only came in children's sizes," she murmured, appreciating Richard's embarrassed flush, which was bright as scarlet and extended to the roots of his sexy, tousled hair.

He sputtered a moment. "I have no quarrel with the equipment, only the prudence of operating it in a public park and terrorizing those using walkways for the intended purpose."

"Which is?"

"Walking."

"Ah." Standing, C.J. retrieved a dog biscuit from her pocket, flipped it to Rags, who leapt up to snag the treat in midair. "It's all right, Richard. I understand."

He angled a wary glance. "You understand what?"

"There's no shame in being afraid."

"Afraid?" He shifted an embarrassed glance toward his daughter. "I am *not* afraid."

C.J. patted his arm. "It's my mistake. I thought everyone knew how to skate. I should have asked."

"Oh, really—"

The indignant sputter was cut off when Lissa called out, "It's easy, Daddy. Watch me." Flushed with excitement, the child eased forward, her stiff torso jerking as she rolled a few feet through the parking lot. She toe-stopped, rotated her arms for balance, then tossed a triumphant look over her shoulder as Rags dashed over, barking. "See?"

"Very nice, punkin." Richard smiled at his daughter, then glowered at C.J., who presumed he'd accepted the gauntlet of her deliberate taunt. "I'll have you know that when I was Lissa's age, I was the speed-skating champion of my block."

"Really?" She managed an innocent gaze. "Then maybe you can teach us a thing or two. Of course, you'll have to put the skates on first."

Eyes darting like those of a cornered cat, Richard heaved a resigned sigh, propped a neatly muscled hip against the van and donned the hated skates, muttering. "In the past three weeks, I've been terrorized by a snake, had my head bashed on a log, was nearly swept out to sea so superdog could go windsurfing—"

C.J. interrupted. "It wasn't Rags's fault the tide came in while you were asleep on the beach."

"And ended up swallowing half of Lake Elsinore trying to keep up with a four-legged, waterskiing showoff." He tightened his lace with a grunt, jammed the helmet on his head and gave C.J. a black stare. "I should have known I was in trouble when I spotted that championship medal pinned to his doggy life vest."

"Oh, that wasn't a waterskiing medal. Rags won the national obedience trials a couple years ago. Don't forget the elbow and knee pads. Safety first." Stifling a smile, C.J. pulled a package of snack crackers out of her own fanny pack, then turned toward Lissa, who was struggling to skate while Rags circled, yelping encouragement. "Lissa, would you put Rags's leash on him, please?"

"Ragsy doesn't need a leash. He follows me real good now."

True enough, since Lissa had proven an apt student,

soaking up every lesson C.J. had offered about training and controlling her mischievous pet. "I know, honey, but this is a public park and dogs aren't allowed unless they're leashed."

The child grumbled, but complied.

"There," Richard said, wobbling upright with a sour look on his face. "Do I pass inspection?"

C.J. nearly choked on a cracker. Helmeted, with his extremities padded and his quivering ankles bowed, the poor man looked so utterly miserable that she almost regretted her part in the rollerblade outing. Still, there was something about a man in spandex Speedos…

Her breath rolled out in a sigh. "Oh, yeah. You pass inspection, and then some."

He grunted, picked his way across the striped asphalt toward the center of the quiet lot, where his daughter had just completed her leashing chore. "Your left boot lace is untied, punkin. Better fix it so you don't trip." Richard might have knelt to assist the child, but Lissa thrust the dog's leash into his hand, then crouched to complete the task herself.

From her vantage point, C.J. watched, smiling and nibbling crackers. A quick glance at her watch, a mental calculation as to the time her next meal would be required, and she was free to focus concentration on the man and child who had become more important to her over the past month than she would ever have dreamed possible.

Lissa had blossomed, becoming more enthusiastic, more exuberant by the day. Fun was no longer something other people enjoyed, people who were viewed through a pane of glass from the isolation of a lonely room. Lissa was outside the window now, having her own fun, participating in her own life.

C.J. was proud of the child, but it was Richard on whom her admiration truly focused. It was he who'd changed the most, allowing his precious daughter the freedom she sought despite his own fear for her safety. He was, C.J. decided, the most special person she'd ever met, a man both loving and strong, with the unique ability to be decisive, yet flexible.

He was also the sexiest, most attractive male on the face of the planet. The sight of that tight, round derriere defined by sleek, elastic bike pants was enough to raise her blood pressure twenty points.

So far, their relationship hadn't progressed beyond the smoldering-glance stage, which was certainly more his choice than hers. C.J. was seriously smitten. If Richard had so much as crooked a pinky finger in her direction, she'd have latched on to him like a starving bug.

But he hadn't crooked a finger, or anything else. Every time she'd thought—no, she'd *known* that he wanted to touch her, to kiss her, a shadow of doubt had darkened his eyes. He'd turned away, leaving C.J. frustrated and confused, wondering why it mattered so much to her. Why *he* mattered so much.

She didn't have an answer. She only knew that Richard did matter, more than she cared to admit.

Across the parking lot, Lissa had finished tying one lace and was checking the other while Rags, clearly perturbed by the leash, paced beside Richard, whining pitifully. C.J. called out to them. "Are you guys about ready?"

Richard glanced up. "Almost."

C.J. tossed the last cracker into her mouth, and was brushing the crumbs from her palms when she noticed a telltale perk of doggy ears. The animal stiffened, bright little eyes focused on a grassy area just beyond the park entrance sign, a wide, double-posted wooden barrier that was three feet high and about five feet long.

The shaggy pooch quivered in excitement just as C.J. spotted the source of his interest, a fuzzy-tailed gray squirrel scampering toward a nearby oak.

C.J. knew in an instant what the devilish dog had in mind, but her warning shout was muffled by a spray of wet cracker crumbs.

It was too little, too late.

Rags yelped, leapt forward. The tightened leash spun Richard around. He grunted, rotating his arms as the slick wheels lurched under his feet.

C.J. pressed her fingers to her mouth, desperately tried to whistle a command. All that emerged was a thin "psfffft," and more wet crumbs.

With a gleeful howl, Rags sprinted across the parking lot like a furry ski boat, dragging the helpless man, who flew across the slick asphalt, bellowing at the top of his lungs.

Lissa jumped up, hollering. "Daddy, let go of the leash!"

But as Richard shrieked by with skate wheels blurred by speed, C.J. saw the leather leash loop encircling his wrist. She swallowed frantically, tried another whistle. "Psfffft."

The alarmed squirrel scampered toward a drooping oak limb with the yelping dog in hot pursuit, and the screaming man zooming across the parking lot. As dog and man headed straight toward the park entrance sign, beside which a meandering path was surrounded with lush green lawn, C.J. frantically skated after them, hoping that once Richard's wheels hit grass, the increased friction would stop his forward momentum.

But Rags had other ideas, and aimed for the sign as if planning to duck under it. Instead, the animal veered at the last minute.

Veering, however, was not a part of Richard's limited skate repertoire. He plowed into the waist-high wooden barrier at full speed with a sound like a fastball slamming a leather catcher's mitt, then did a rather nicely executed head flip and landed in a crumpled heap on the other side.

"Oh, God!" C.J. rolled around the sign, knelt by the man who was red faced and gasping. "Richard! Are you all right?" When he gurgled, she saw his arm twisted oddly, and the leash wrapped around his neck. At the other end of the leash, Rags yipped and strained as his fuzzy adversary scampered up the tree.

C.J. whistled. The animal peered over his shoulder with a tongue-lolling grin. C.J. snapped a hand signal. His ears drooped. She signaled again and he slunk over, bellied beside her, loosening the leash enough for her to free the gasping man.

Air rushed into Richard's lungs with a tortured rush. She cradled his red face in her hands. "Are you hurt? Can you move your arms? Can you see, can you speak, have you broken any bones? Oh, Lord, I'm so sorry—"

He shuddered, opened an eye. "Are we having fun yet?"

Limp with relief, she sat back on her heels, babbling

wildly. "I'm so sorry, so very, very sorry. I tried to stop him, honest I did, but I was eating crackers and I couldn't whistle, so Rags kept running, and you kept screaming, and I kept spitting crumbs, and I was so afraid you were going to break your neck, and—"

"Do you still have crackers in your mouth?"

"Ah, no."

"Good."

Richard reached up so quickly the movement was a blur, cupped the back of her helmeted head and brought her mouth down to his in a kiss so passionate that she melted across his chest like warm butter.

His lips were moist, hot, so demanding that she felt helpless to quell the electric surge skimming her spine, numbing her extremities. Muscles quivered, breath ceased, hearts raced with enough power to vibrate bones and heat pulsing blood to a boil. She tasted him, a heavy sweetness that touched her to the core, ignited a torch of need so intense that her mind spun without thought or focus, overwhelmed by the purity of sensation, of taste and touch, of moist heat and salty-sweet tang, of masculine musk mingled with deep, probing promise.

Blood roared past her ears, muffling sound. From a distance, C.J. heard something familiar. A voice, perhaps. She ignored it, focused only on the plethora of sensations coursing through her quivering body, paralyzing her dizzy mind.

The voice was closer now, more desperate. "Daddy!"

Before C.J.'s stunned brain could react, something hit with the force of a body blow, knocking her backward.

"Daddy, Daddy!"

Levering up on one elbow, C.J. shook her head,

blinked and saw Lissa kneeling beside her father, shaking him by the shirt. "Breathe, Daddy, breathe!"

Richard, eyes rolling from being so violently shaken, sucked a ragged breath.

"You're alive!" Lissa shouted an inch from his startled face, then flung herself across his chest, sobbing in relief.

Clearly bewildered, Richard patted his daughter's back, flinched as he pushed upright into a sitting position. "Hey, punkin, everything is all right."

Sniffing, Lissa sat back, wiped her wet eyes. "I thought you died like Mommy."

A veil of cautious misery darkened his gaze. "Why would you think that, sweetheart?"

"'Cause C.J. was doing that CPR stuff to you."

Richard's eyes opened wide, darted a guilty glance in C.J.'s direction. "Umm, well, actually—"

"Teacher showed us how to do it," Lissa said firmly. "She told us whenever people stop breathing and stuff, we hafta breathe for them so they won't die." A fresh spurt of tears coursed down her cheeks. "I don't want you to die, Daddy."

C.J. felt her face heat, then cool as her gaze met Richard's. She puffed her cheeks, blew out a breath and issued a limp shrug.

He cleared his throat, took his daughter's hands. "I'm not going to die, Lissa. I'm not even hurt."

The child angled a perplexed glance at C.J. "Then why was she doing CPR stuff?"

"Well, she wasn't, actually. I, ah, that is, we were, well, kissing."

Lissa blinked numbly, comprehension seeping slowly

into hazel eyes that turned darker and greener by the moment. "Kissing?" She pivoted on her knees, scowling darkly. "You were kissing *my daddy?*"

C.J. tried for a smile, settled for a nod.

The girl's eyes narrowed into mean green slits. "Why?"

"Well, ah, because he'd just fallen down and he looked like he needed a kiss."

If looks were weapons, Lissa's razor-sharp glare would have drawn blood. She yanked the leash loop off her father's wrist, huffed into a standing position and stomped her skated feet across the grass toward the path, yanking the leash when Rags stoically remained in his commanded position.

C.J. snapped her fingers, and the released animal promptly jumped up to follow Lissa while casting worried glances over his little dog shoulder.

Richard heaved a sigh, brushed the grass off his knees, then squinted up with a thin smile. "That went well, don't you think?"

"You don't want to know what I think."

He stroked the back of C.J.'s hand with his thumb. "She'll come around."

"And if she doesn't?"

Richard glanced away. He didn't answer. He didn't have to.

Lissa was the most important person in Richard's life. There was nothing he wouldn't do to keep her safe, to make her happy. If it came down to a choice between his daughter's happiness and his own, there wasn't a doubt in the world which he would choose.

Logically C.J. understood that, even admired it. She'd

never wanted, nor would she ever allow herself, to become a wedge between father and daughter, even if it meant removing herself from their lives—and Rags's life—completely.

Deep down, she'd always suspected it might come to that. She just hadn't realized how much it would hurt.

PLAY "LUCKY 7" AND GET
THREE FREE GIFTS!

HOW TO PLAY:

1. With a coin, carefully scratch off the silver box at the right. Then check the claim c
to see what we have for you — **FREE BOOKS** and a gift — **ALL YOURS! ALL FRE**

2. Send back this card and you'll receive brand-new Silhouette Romance® novels. The
books have a cover price of $3.50 each, but they are yours to keep absolutely free.

3. There's no catch. You're under no obligation to buy anything. We charge nothing
ZERO — for your first ship
And you don't have to ma
any minimum number of
purchases — not even or

4. The fact is thousands of readers enjoy receiving books by mail from the Silhouett
Reader Service™ months before they're available in stores. They like the convenience
home delivery and they love our discount prices!

5. We hope that after receiving your free books you'll want to remain a subscriber. B
the choice is yours — to continue or cancel, any time at all! So why not take us up c
invitation, with no risk of any kind. You'll be glad you did!

YOURS FREE!

PLAY LUCKY 7 FOR THIS EXCITING FREE GIFT!

*THIS SURPRISE
MYSTERY GIFT
COULD BE
YOURS FREE WHEN
YOU PLAY*

LUCKY 7!

©1990 HARLEQUIN ENTERPRISES LIMITED

NO COST! NO OBLIGATION TO BUY!
NO PURCHASE NECESSARY!

PLAY THE

LUCKY 7 SLOT MACHINE GAME!

Just scratch off the silver box with a coin. Then check below to see the gifts you get!

YES!

I have scratched off the silver box. Please send me all the gifts for which I qualify. I understand I am under no obligation to purchase any books, as explained on the back and on the opposite page.

215 SDL CGU3
(U-SIL-R-07/98)

Name _____

PLEASE PRINT CLEARLY

Address _____ Apt.# _____

City _____ State _____ Zip _____

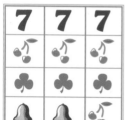

WORTH TWO FREE BOOKS PLUS A BONUS MYSTERY GIFT!

WORTH TWO FREE BOOKS!

WORTH ONE FREE BOOK!

TRY AGAIN!

Offer limited to one per household and not valid to current Silhouette Romance® subscribers. All orders subject to approval.

PRINTED IN U.S.A.

DETACH AND MAIL CARD TODAY!

The Silhouette Reader Service™ — Here's how it works

Accepting free books places you under no obligation to buy anything. You may keep the books and gift and return the shipping statement marked "cancel." If you do not cancel, about a month later we'll send you 6 additional novels, and bill you just $2.90 each, plus 25¢ delivery per book and applicable sales tax, if any.* That's the complete price — and compared to cover prices of $3.50 each — quite a bargain! You may cancel at any time, but if you choose to continue, every month we'll send you 6 more books, which you may either purchase at the discount price...or return to us and cancel your subscription.

*Terms and prices subject to change without notice. Sales tax applicable in N.Y.

BUSINESS REPLY MAIL
FIRST-CLASS MAIL   PERMIT NO. 717   BUFFALO, NY

POSTAGE WILL BE PAID BY ADDRESSEE

SILHOUETTE READER SERVICE
3010 WALDEN AVE
PO BOX 1867
BUFFALO NY 14240-9952

NO POSTAGE
NECESSARY
IF MAILED
IN THE
UNITED STATES

Chapter Six

"One hot dog with the works and an extra large soda." Richard passed the cardboard carrier to Lissa, who eagerly scootched across the grass to accept it. "And one unsweetened iced tea."

C.J., who'd consumed her own packed lunch an hour earlier, took the icy drink with a grateful smile. "Where's yours?"

"I, ah, ate it." With an endearing sheepish shrug, he shifted the rollerblades, which had been tied by the laces and draped over his shoulder. "I figured it would be easier to carry in my stomach." He slipped a nervous glance at Lissa, who'd pinched the end off her hot dog and was offering it to Rags. "Ah, everything okay, punkin?"

The child shrugged. "Not enough ketchup." Richard flinched a bit, but said nothing more. C.J.'s heart went out to both of them. She knew that Richard wasn't asking about the hot dog he'd retrieved from the park's snack stand. Lissa had been sullen and visibly aggravated since the unfortunate kissing encounter this morning. So sullen, in fact, that Richard had seemed hesitant to leave her and C.J. alone long enough to fetch his daughter's lunch.

"Everything is fine, Richard. Lissa and I just sat here quietly enjoying the nice view."

"Oh. That's nice." The disappointment in his eyes revealed that he understood her meaning. Lissa still wasn't speaking to her. Clearly, he was distressed by that.

C.J. was, too.

Richard glanced around, rubbed his palms on his spandex-clad thighs. "Well, in that case…" The words trailed off as he gazed down the gentle slope to a woodsy outbuilding barely visible among the trees. "I'll, ah, be back in a few minutes."

Lissa swung around, her relish-smeared cheeks bulging. "Where are you going?" The question was muffled, but audible.

"Er, to the rest room."

"Oh." Satisfied, she swallowed, wiped her mouth with her sleeve and bit off another healthy bite as her father trudged down the hill. Beside her, Rags pawed her arm, whining. "No," she said firmly enough to spray crumbs. "You've had enough."

Rags sighed, cast a hopeful eye toward C.J., who dug into her pocket for a dog biscuit.

Lissa skewered her with a look. "I said he's had enough."

"Ah. Of course." Angling an apologetic glance at the disappointed animal, C.J. pocketed the biscuit, leaned against the rough bark of a gnarled oak old enough to have sheltered weary travelers for centuries. Some cultures believed that ancient trees were vessels of wisdom, absorbing the knowledge of ages, and storing it in the growth rings hidden deep inside pulpy cores. C.J. could have used some of that wisdom about now.

The breeze, soft as warm cotton, brushed her cheek. C.J. closed her eyes, remembering her own childhood, when the face in her mirror had been so similar to Lissa's.

One specific day had been much like this one, a beautiful Sunday, mild and clear, with puffy clouds shuttering distant mountain peaks. C.J. could recall seeing those mountains from her bedroom window, just as she had seen her beloved father romping with her siblings.

Sunday had been Daddy's only day off, a few precious hours in which to bestow revered attention upon a gaggle of children hungry for it. C.J. had been hungry for it, too, but she was confined to her sickroom, isolated and alone. Gazing outside, she'd watched her father scoop up her older sister to whirl the laughing girl over his head. C.J.'s flat little chest had hurt so much she'd nearly cried.

She still remembered the pain, the jealousy that had sawed like sharp teeth into her heart. She remembered everything she'd seen that day, everything she'd felt. She remembered how desperately she'd wanted her father's attention. But most of all, she remembered the decision she'd made to get that attention, a choice that would haunt her the rest of her life.

A sound brought her back to the present. C.J. blinked, realized that Lissa was speaking. "Do you got a tummy ache or something?"

"No, I feel fine, honey. Why?"

She shrugged. "I dunno. You just looked kind of sad."

"Oh." C.J. forced a smile. "I must have been day-dreaming."

Lissa nodded, reached out to stroke Rags's shaggy head. "I guess he can have one."

"Have one?"

The girl angled a hesitant glance. "You know, a doggy treat. I mean, if you still want to give him one, it's okay with me."

Recognizing the gesture as a peace offering, C.J. dug into her pocket. Rags, alert to the tasty transaction, perked up instantly as C.J. handed all the treats over to Lissa, passing over more than dog biscuits. She was also bestowing full ownership and control to the child, who cupped her hands to accept the gift with eyes clouded by confusion. "You keep them," C.J. told her. "That way Rags will learn that he has to ask you for his treats, and you can decide when you want him to have one."

Lissa looked down at the pile of bone-shaped biscuits in her palms, then up at C.J. Confusion melted into comprehension, and a moist sheen prickled her young eyes. "Okay." She shifted, allowed C.J. to open the pocket of her shorts so she could deposit all but one of the treats, which she promptly pitched toward the eager animal. Rags snagged it midair, ate it in a single bite, then stood at alert, quivering in anticipation.

Grinning, Lissa retrieved another and another. Just as C.J. worried that the child would allow the animal to consume the entire stash, Lissa brushed her palms together. "That's all, Ragsy. Go lie down."

Rags heaved a contented sigh, and did so.

As Lissa slid C.J. a sideways glance, her smile dimmed to a wary grimace. She squirmed, nervously scratched at her bare knee. "You gonna come to my birthday next week?"

"Do you want me to?"

"Yeah, I guess so." Another glance, another restless wriggle. "If you want to."

"I honestly can't think of anything I'd rather do," C.J. whispered, opening her arms. The child hesitated only a moment before scrambling into the proffered embrace and hugging her fiercely. A lump rose in C.J.'s throat as the sweet scent of strawberry shampoo wafted from Lissa's braided hair. The warmth of a child in her arms, the ache of an empty heart being filled too full, too fast.

C.J. understood this child, and loved her desperately. The feeling was awesome, unbearably intense. It scared her half to death.

From the base of the hill, Richard watched the tender scene with his own sense of awe. That's what his daughter had been missing all these years, a woman's touch, a mother's love, the emotional connection that even the most determined father could never quite achieve.

C.J. had achieved it. She'd instinctively seen what was needed, had simply opened her arms. An offer of love. So basic, so simple, yet so precious and rare.

Something inside his chest cracked. The sensation unnerved him, made him catch his breath. He didn't understand what was happening to him, or to his child, but he knew it was wonderful.

Their lives had been irrevocably changed. That, too, was wonderful.

Richard adjusted the magnifying light, hunched over the dismantled clock, pieces of which were strewn across the dining-room table. Using tweezers, he seated a tiny gear in place, tightened a holding screw with a tool resembling a miniature screwdriver. He adjusted the tiny counterweight until the teeth of the newly seated gear meshed with the cogwheel. The clock ticked. It was out of sync, of course. He'd have to tweak the timing mechanism, fine-tune the ratchet. That was his favorite part of the process. The devil was in the details, after all. Richard liked details.

He shifted in the chair, massaging the back of his neck and the dull ache spreading across his shoulders. The click of doggy toenails caught his attention as Rags wandered from the kitchen, his shaggy beard dripping.

"Got yourself a bedtime drink, hmm?"

Rags yawned, cast a sanguine eye toward the hallway, alerting Richard to the sound of his daughter's voice emanating from the fluffy gingham bedroom. She was engaged in quiet conversation, not unusual in itself except that the furry coconspirator to whom she usually vocalized her thoughts was scratching himself in the kitchen doorway.

Richard stretched, rose from the chair and wandered toward his daughter's room.

"So you mustn't ever worry," she was saying with great solemnity. "Your daddy loves you more than anyone in the whole entire world."

Frowning, Richard softened his step, peeked cautiously through the open door. There, in the center of a semicircle of puppets arranged on the carpeted floor, sat Lissa using a wizard hand puppet to carry on discussion with the droopy Pinocchio that had been propped against the base of her nightstand.

Her voice rose to a squeak as she mimicked Pinocchio's response. "But what if he loves someone better?"

The bearded puppet wiggled on her hand, and her voice lowered to wizard tenor. "Daddies have room to love lots of people, just like doggies do, but they never, ever love anybody as much as they love their children."

"But what if I do something really bad, and he goes away?" Lissa-as-Pinocchio squeaked.

"Daddies never go away," she insisted, wiggling her hand puppet, then answered herself, squeaking, "Sometimes they do. There's lots of kids in class who never, ever see their daddies, and they're really sad."

"Your daddy would never leave you," Lissa-the-wizard replied. "He loves you lots more than your mommy did, 'cause she went away and he didn't."

Richard backed away from the door, took a moment to compose himself. A deep breath, then another. It was true, he thought, and couldn't believe why he hadn't realized before how desperately Lissa wanted a mother. *Needed* a mother.

But not just any mother.

With a final breath, Richard cleared his throat, stepped into the open doorway. "It's bedtime, punkin."

She glanced up, seemed unconcerned by his appearance. "Okay."

He started to speak again, but the words clogged in his throat. He coughed them away as Lissa gathered her puppets and replaced them lovingly on the shelves. After a moment, he tried again. "You like C.J., don't you, punkin?"

Her shoulders stiffened slightly, and her hand hovered a moment longer than necessary before she scooped up a feathered owl puppet and settled the toy on a nearby chair. "C.J. is my friend."

Relief poured warmly through his torso, released by his own knowing smile. It was the assurance he'd wanted to hear, what he'd needed to hear, what he'd expected to hear. Perhaps that's why he paid so little attention to his daughter's emphasis on the word *my*.

It was an omission he'd come to regret.

Bobbi glanced up from scooping a warm batch of chocolate chip cookies from baking sheet to cooling rack. "Are you sure you don't want to slip into that sexy silk pants suit you bought last week?"

"For the third time, no. I'm perfectly comfortable."

Bobbi dropped the spatula to pile doughy mixing bowls in the sink. "Don't you take pride in your appearance?"

"Huh?" Startled, C.J. glanced down at her beloved sweats, topped by her favorite T-shirt, a stretched and scroungy screen-print proclaiming that Dancers Do It With Their Toes. "What's wrong with my appearance?"

"You look a scrunge."

"So what? As soon as I finish balancing the studio books I plan to look like a scrunge in pajamas."

"Pajamas? No, no, no, absolutely not, uh-uh, completely unacceptable." Clucking madly, Bobbi scurried over so quickly that her spectacles slipped down her substantial nose. She shoved them back in place, fixed C.J. with a bright-eyed grin. "I mean, it's not even dinnertime and you're talking pajamas. You sound like an old spinster."

"I *am* an old spinster."

"Gimme a break. You're twenty-eight."

"That's old. Anyway, it feels old." Heaving a sigh, C.J. flopped onto the sofa, kicked her bare feet onto the coffee table, beside one of her roommate's cameras and a scattered pile of film. "All I want to do is finish my bookkeeping, crawl into my favorite chair, make popcorn and settle down to watch a good flick on TV." From the corner of her eye C.J. saw her roommate cast an anxious glance at the clock. "What time are you meeting Maury?"

"Hmm? Oh. In a while." Frowning, Bobbi returned to the kitchen to pack some of the cooled cookies into a plastic container.

"Those for Maury?"

"Of course. You know what they say about the way to a man's heart being through his stomach."

"I always heard it was lower."

Bobbi's chuckle was cut off by the doorbell. "Oops. Gotta go." She jammed the lid on the cookie container, snagged her purse off the kitchen table and headed for the front door.

"Have a good time," C.J. said, surprised Maury was calling for his longtime girlfriend at the apartment rather than meeting her downtown as was his habit.

Juggling the cookies, Bobbi grasped the knob, angled a smug grin over her shoulder. "You too, hon." With that, she yanked open the door. "Hey, there! Whoa, not bad, not bad at all. Yes, indeedy, I *do* approve. Come on in, handsome. Take a load off. Ceejz, company!"

C.J. stiffened, whipped a stunned glance over her shoulder and nearly fainted as Richard Matthews, holding a bouquet of red roses and dressed to the nines, was practically yanked into the room by her grinning roommate. "What on earth—?"

"Have fun, you two! Catch you later."

By the time C.J. lurched to her feet, Bobbi was gone and Richard was standing there with a shell-shocked expression that would have been comical under other circumstances. His stunned gaze swept C.J.'s casual attire, pausing midchest to either read her shirt or study its less than admirable contours, then sliding down to the torn sweatpants and bare feet. "Ah...am I early?"

"Early for what?"

He blinked, licked his lips. "Our reservations aren't for another half hour."

"Reservations?"

His shoulders sagged as he cast a weary glance out to the empty hallway down which Bobbi had just disappeared. "I take it you didn't get my message."

Puffing her cheeks, C.J. blew out a breath, jammed a fist on her hip and tapped her foot. "I will kill her, that's all there is to it, I'm going to murder that sneaky roommate of mine in her sleep."

"Oh." Richard shifted, glanced around the cluttered apartment, then down at the flowers he held. "Then I guess we'd better put these in water, although they'll be pretty well wilted by the time you finish doing twenty-five to life."

"Justifiable homicide." C.J. crossed the room, took the roses with a grateful smile. "No jury on earth will convict me."

Richard returned her smile, albeit nervously. "She said you'd be ready by six."

"My roommate has a twisted sense of humor." C.J. inhaled the sweet fragrance, carried the bouquet into the kitchen and was arranging them in a vase when Richard joined her. The confusion in his eyes made her heart ache with peculiar guilt.

"I don't understand," he said quietly. "When I called this afternoon to see if you were free for dinner, why didn't your roommate—Bobbi, isn't it?" He acknowledged C.J.'s nod. "Why didn't Bobbi simply give you my message?"

"Because she knew I would have refused." Avoiding his gaze, C.J. fiddled with the flowers, cursing her own foolishness in having confided in a woman born with a megaphone in her mouth. "That is, I, er, have bookkeeping to do."

Not exactly a fabrication, even though the complexity of her own feelings for Richard, and for Lissa as well, weighed heavily on C.J.'s mind, even more heavily on her heart. She thought of them constantly, reliving moments from their times together with warmth and a secret smile, or anticipating their next meeting with such nervous expectation that sometimes she couldn't even sleep from the excitement.

In the past weeks, Richard and Lissa had become such an important part of C.J.'s world she could barely remember what life was like before she'd met them. That worried her. And it frightened her, too, because her emotions had spiraled out of control. To C.J. control was everything.

Richard cleared his throat. "Well, I guess I should go. I'm sorry for the mistake."

"Wait." She met his gaze, was instantly swept up in the power, the intensity, the generated heat. He looked so bewildered, so sad. So vulnerable. It was all she could do to keep herself from touching his freshly shaved chin, from pressing her palm against his dear face and whispering that there was nothing on earth she wanted more than to spend every evening of her life with him, and only with him.

But how could she express something that she herself couldn't accept, or even understand?

She moistened her lips, nodded at the rest of the cooling cookies. "Would you like to take some home for Lissa? I'm told they're quite good."

"Lissa's not home. She spends Friday nights with her grandparents." His telling smile didn't escape C.J.'s notice, nor did the realization that this was indeed Friday night.

"Cookies keep. She can have some tomorrow."

"Lissa's allergic to chocolate."

"Oh. I didn't know."

Shifting uncomfortably, Richard used a fingertip to stroke a velvet rose pedal. "She's allergic to a lot of things, but chocolate gives her a particularly violent reaction."

"That makes two of us," C.J. murmured, her gaze riveted on his sensual caress, the slow, delicate slide of his fingertip along the soft, floral curves. "I can't have chocolate, either."

"Too bad." He helped himself to a cookie, took a slow, melting bite. "Food of the gods."

"Yes." It came out on a sigh. She reached out to wipe a crumb from his lips. "Better than sex." Her eyes widened in horror. Had she actually said that out loud?

Richard's startled stare indicated she most certainly had said it, but there was no time to be mortified. Richard was choking. She whacked his back with the flat of her hand. He gurgled. She whacked harder, then spun and filled a glass with tap water.

He waved it away, gasping and red faced. "No... thanks. I'm fine." He coughed, wheezed and straightened, brushing his lapels in that endearing manner indicative of one trying to recoup a modicum of dignity. "Well, I should leave you to, er, your work." A strained smile, an appealing nod, and he pivoted sharply.

"Five minutes," C.J. heard herself say.

He jerked to a stop, gazed over his shoulder as if certain he'd misheard. "Pardon me?"

"Just let me change clothes, take an insulin booster and I'll be ready to rock-and-roll."

A flicker of hope melted the final trace of her resistance. "Are you sure? I mean, only if you want to."

At that moment, there was nothing on earth C.J. wanted more.

"I'm so sorry. I don't know what got into me."

"It's all right," Richard mumbled, sloshing across the parking lot. "I should have known better than trying to pick a water lily bloom—" he gave her a narrowed stare "—as a romantic memento for an ungrateful woman."

"I'm not ungrateful." She bit back a smile as his leather shoes squeaked with every step. "It was a lovely gesture, truly it was. I was really quite touched."

"You have a peculiar way of displaying it."

"But when I leaned over your shoulder and saw that huge koi swimming toward your hand, I thought it was going to bite you."

"So naturally you chose to increase the odds?"

"I didn't mean to push you in. I, er, tripped. After all, I got wet, too."

His gaze settled on the few stray water spots dampening her apple green silk top. "How tragic for you."

C.J. tried not to laugh. She really did. But he looked so, well, adorably piqued that she couldn't help herself.

Richard hiked a brow, feigned an indignation betrayed by the merest flicker of amusement in his eyes. "I'm so pleased you're enjoying yourself. It's almost worth destruction of a two-hundred-dollar suit just to hear the soothing strains of your delighted laughter."

C.J. balled a fist in front of her quivering mouth, but her struggle for composure ended in an unladylike snort that tickled her immensely. She turned away, chuckling madly, and finally reined in her amusement long enough to speak. "I truly am sorry, Richard. It really was an accident. When I saw that huge fish open a mouth the size of Kansas and head straight for your hand, the image of you trying to rebuild a clock with your teeth flashed into my mind." She angled a glance, nearly lost it as a rivulet of water rolled smoothly from a curled forelock to drip off his nose. Her lips quivered. "I mean, haven't you ever seen *Jaws?*"

"Ah, yes. Terrifying movie." A grave nod, a somber frown. "And I certainly understand how a fat goldfish in a fountain pond could reasonably be mistaken for a twenty-foot man-eater."

"It was a *very* fat goldfish."

"Very."

"And the light was extremely dim."

"Extremely."

The corner of his mouth quirked, as if reluctant to release a struggling smile. A sweet warmth melted inside her chest, a buttery softness that caressed her heart even as it squeezed the breath from her lungs. The amber glow of security lights illuminated the strength of his jaw, the gentle curve of lips too vulnerable to be masculine, bracketed by deep, manly grooves that her fingers itched to touch.

Odd that she hadn't noticed that dichotomy before, the soft eyes and gentle mouth outlined by rugged creases and jutting planes of distinctive strength that was undeniably male.

Details caught her eye. A vague blemish above brows too straight to be fashionable, with stray hairs wandering across the bridge of an appealing if slightly imperfect nose. Deep-set eyes, lids shadowed by midnight darkness even as overhead illumination accented a distinguishing ridge of brow and bone, a surprising contrast of sharp planes and softness that was unique to this man.

He shifted beneath her gaze. A shoulder shrugged. The damp suit coat slipped off to reveal a silken shirt clinging to the contours of a chest she suddenly longed to stroke. He flipped the coat over his shoulder, turned his face away to gaze across the sea of glimmering automobiles. "Where did we park, anyway?"

"Hmm?" She blinked, absently clutched her swaying stomach. "Ah, by a tree, I think."

"That narrows it down," he murmured with a smile.

Tearing her attention from the rapt study of his features, she realized that every space in the lot was accented by a sapling swaying in the soft summer breeze.

Her mind was a complete blank. She couldn't remember anything about their arrival except that she'd been fascinated by a gleam of moisture gathering on Richard's upper lip as they'd pulled in, and hadn't been able to take her eyes off his face as they'd walked to the restaurant.

"We can just wander around until we find it," she suggested, pleased by the thought that the car search would add to their time together. "The air is warm enough to dry you off a bit."

His gaze slipped suggestively from her eyes, traveling down her body with an appreciative glint that made her shiver. "I can think of more pleasant places to dry off."

So could C.J. The steamy image weakened her knees. When they finally buckled, Richard dropped the wet suit coat and pulled her into his arms. Her palms flattened against his chest, tingled with warmth oozing from beneath the silky shirt fabric. The beat of his heart joined her own racing pulse. Her fingers coiled, were rewarded by his erotic quiver.

His lips slackened, then tensed.

Her legs trembled.

The night air encircled them like loving arms, soft, sensuous, floating on scents that aroused the senses, boggled her swirling mind. Sweet jasmine mingled with the musky fragrance of expensive cologne. The subtle tang of a distant ocean, a whiff of tempting smoke from a charcoal grill, the essence of wet wool and masculine arousal, an olfactory smorgasbord that overwhelmed the senses, left C.J. breathless and shaken.

Richard, too, was affected. His breath came sharply, in shallow puffs, one after another. "You look beautiful tonight."

"So do you." On some level, she understood the foolishness of her response, but couldn't dwell on that because Richard was caressing her bare arms with such delicious sensation that she could barely breathe, let alone think.

"I want to kiss you," he murmured.

She knew that. "Why don't you?"

"The moment has to be perfect."

"It doesn't get more perfect than this."

"We're in a parking lot."

"A very romantic parking lot."

"You're standing on my coat."

"A lovely gesture." She pushed his necktie aside, popped a button on his shirt, slipped her fingers under the fabric to caress his warm flesh. "I've always wanted a man to lay down his coat for me."

Richard shivered at her touch, lowered his head until his lips were millimeters from her own. "Just call me Sir Walter," he murmured against her mouth, then took it with a sweetness that drained the strength from her spine.

She sagged against him, molded herself to every nuance of his body until his heart pounded against hers, and the rising strength at the apex of his thighs pressed against the melting core of her femininity. Lights flashed in her mind. Bells whistled through her brain. Her limp body sprang to life as if erotically charged.

Flinging her arms around his neck, she wrestled him closer, parting her lips with sensual invitation. He accepted eagerly, moaning, and fused his lips to her mouth while his hands grappled with her sleeveless silk tunic.

They spun around, panting and groping, bounced off the side of one car to splay across the hood of another. Lips tasted, tongues touched, hands grasped, skin shivered. Breath came in ragged gasps, steamed by the humid air. Beneath them the bouncing vehicle shuddered, beeped, then let out a piercing wail that had them leaping apart like guilty adolescents.

C.J. spun around, disoriented and dizzy, while Richard gaped in horror at the screeching car.

"Shh." He touched a finger to his lips, then patted the hood as if trying to calm a distressed child. "Shh, quiet." The car siren wailed even louder. "Oh, Lord." His frantic gaze encircled the parking lot, settled on a shadowed group emerging from a nearby boutique. A buzz of worried voices was vaguely discernible beyond the din of the car alarm.

Richard snatched the trampled coat with one hand, grabbed C.J.'s wrist with the other. They sprinted across the parking lot like fleeing felons to crouch behind a minivan parked at the far end of the lot. Catching her breath, C.J. peeked around the van's hood, saw the shadowed group hustle toward the still-screeching car. She started to giggle.

"Quiet," Richard whispered, although he, too, was struggling with a chuckle. "Unless you really want to explain to those nice people what we were doing on the hood of their shiny new car."

An uncontrollable giggle ended in a hiccup. C.J. covered her mouth, fought the bubbling laughter. "How much time would we do for contributing to the delinquency of a Buick?''

Richard's snort of laughter was cut off by two sharp beeps emanating from the far end of the lot, after which the car alarm finally fell silent. He crept along the side of the van, straightened to peer over the hood and whacked the top of his head on the rearview mirror.

C.J. yanked the howling man down, shushing him madly. "Be quiet. Do you want them to hear you?"

"Sorry," he muttered, rubbing his skull. "I'll just crouch here and bleed silently."

"Oh, for goodness sake." She grabbed his ears, jerked his head down to examine the top of his scalp. "You're not bleeding. There's not even a bump."

His head bobbed when she released him. "Gee, what great news. I guess the evening isn't a total bust after all."

"I have even better news." C.J. rose to peer through the van window. "We found your car."

The city spread out in magnificent splendor, a jeweled cape wrapped around the shoulders of midnight.

"It's breathtaking," C.J. whispered.

Beside her, Richard released the steering wheel to touch her hand. "I thought you might like it." Shadows concealed his face, but his handsome features were indelibly etched in her mind. She felt rather than saw his smile as he squeezed her hand, then exited the van.

A moment later, the side door opened. C.J. swiveled in her seat, peered over the backrest. "What are you doing?"

"You'll see." The door slid shut, and a silhouette melted into the trees.

A minute ticked by. Two minutes.

C.J. squinted into the darkness, toward a place where the bluff disappeared into the sequined splendor of the city below. She was so compelled by the breathless beauty of the view that she lost track of time until Richard startled her by opening the passenger door.

"Your carriage awaits, m'lady."

She accepted his hand, allowed him to help her step from the van. "A carriage?"

"Not really a carriage. A sitting area." He guided her down the moonlit path, to a grassy knoll overlooking the city lights.

"Oh..." Overwhelmed, she touched her throat, gazed down at the preparations he'd made. A soft comforter was spread out, with fat throw pillows artistically arranged beside a silver ice bucket in which a magnum of diet ginger ale was chilling. A matching tray held two crystal goblets, along with an assortment of crackers, cheeses and fruit. "This is for me?"

"Of course."

Still holding her hand, he escorted her to the downy nest he'd created, and fluffed a pillow, upon which she reclined with a pampered sigh. "This is so romantic."

Richard stretched out beside her, plucked a grape from the fruit tray. "I aim to please."

C.J. accepted the grape, opening her mouth as he laid it reverently on her tongue, then she snuggled into his arms, rested her head on his shoulder.

The night was magical, wondrous, beyond anything she'd ever experienced. They talked for hours, about their hopes, their dreams, the resilience of children, the fragility of the human soul. They shared moments of their own lives, happy moments, sad moments. They smiled with each other, cried with each other, until the city lights had dimmed to dusky pinpoints, and dawn smeared magenta clouds across a violet sky.

They watched the sunrise as they'd watched the moon fall, wrapped in each other's arms. By the time the jeweled city glowed golden in the morning sun, C.J. Moray was in love.

Chapter Seven

Having entered through the open screen door and laid her gift on the colorful stack in the living room, C.J. tiptoed to the kitchen door, pausing to soak up the sweet sight of a devoted father efficiently icing his daughter's birthday cake. From her vantage point behind Richard, she could see only part of the tasty project as he used a flat implement to swirl frosty pink peaks atop the round layers with practiced skill.

She thought about the many cakes he'd baked alone, the birthdays he'd prepared for the motherless child he so clearly adored. Watching him fidget with decorating details, she felt a surge of admiration, and something more. Something private. Something profound.

C.J. was in awe of Richard, of the responsibilities he shouldered without complaint, the obligations he accepted without protest. Richard Matthews was more than Lissa's father. He was her protector, her mentor, her nurturer and her strength, a man who loved deeply and powerfully, dedicated, committed, unafraid.

Committed.

That single word conveyed the essence of everything Richard stood for, and everything C.J. feared. His promise was an immutable bond, unbendable, unbreakable, unbounded. There were no retreats in Richard's world, no mistakes to be rectified, no miscalculations to be rethought. A vow was a contract, the terms of which must be fulfilled regardless of consequence. He gave all of himself. He expected no less from others.

The assumption that others shared his stoic sense of duty was his greatest weakness, showing the vulnerability of misplaced trust, the blindness of one who refuses to acknowledge the frailty of others. It gave people power to hurt and disappoint.

C.J. feared that she, too, would eventually disappoint him.

But not today. Today her heart swelled with emotion too deep to define, with an ache so sweet that she wanted to shout it from rooftops. Today she was in love. And as always, C.J. never worried about tomorrow. The future would take care of itself.

Silently, stealthily, she slipped across the kitchen, slid her arms around him while hoisted up on tiptoes to nuzzle the back of his neck.

"Umm." A ripple vibrated the muscles of his chest, but he continued fiddling with the cake without missing a beat. "I wondered when you were going to get around to that."

"You heard me come in?"

"Of course." A deft swirl, a final perfectly placed

peak, and he laid the frosting knife aside, turned in the circle of her arms. "My radar is attuned to your every move."

He kissed her then, deeply, sweetly, with an unbridled passion that was shocking, considering the fact that Lissa could walk in on them at any time.

Interruption was the last thing on C.J.'s mind as she clung to him, returning his kiss with a fervor that may have been unwise given the circumstances, but was nonetheless out of her control. She wanted him, all of him. Every time she touched him, held him, kissed him, she was overwhelmed by aching need, a desire so intense that her toes literally curled with it.

When Richard finally released her, his breath came in shallow gulps. He, too, was shaken, but managed a small smile. "Do you like it?"

"Oh, yes," she breathed, shivering as gooseflesh prickled her arms. "I love it."

"You don't think it's too pink, do you?"

A befuddled blink, a startled stare and C.J. realized he was referring to the cake. "Oh. No. Pink is good. Er, is it strawberry or cherry?"

"Strawberry."

She moistened her lips, steadied herself on the kitchen table. "I don't suppose that's sugar-free icing, is it?"

A cloud of regret veiled his eyes. "No, I'm sorry."

"Well, I'll forgive you this time." She angled a sly glance, lifted her lips. "For a price."

"Blackmail, hmm?" He jerked her against his chest, paid her off with another long, slow kiss.

She heaved a shuddering sigh. "More."

As he lowered his head to comply, the thump of running feet in the hallway was punctuated by Lissa's excited shriek. "Gramma and Gramps are here!" A blur of blue gingham flew by the open doorway, followed by the squeak of the front door screen as the child dashed out to greet her grandparents.

Tension revealed itself slowly, creasing its way along his brow. C.J. reluctantly stepped from his arms. "I doubt Mr. McCade will be pleased to see me here."

"Lissa wants you here. That's all that matters."

"And you?"

A quick smile. "I always want you."

"Good answer."

"I can't wait until Lissa sees your present."

"Do you think she'll like it? I mean, I haven't actually heard her say that it's something she wants...."

Words ceased as Richard gently stroked her cheek with his thumb. "Trust me, she'll be thrilled."

Before C.J. could reply, her attention was diverted by commotion from the other room, Lissa's happy chatter along with Thompson McCade's booming voice. Rags slunk into the kitchen, whining.

Richard absently bent to scratch the dog's head, then straightened, smoothed the front of his stylish knit golf shirt as if wiping away telltale remnants of their shared intimacy. "I should greet them." He sounded apologetic.

"Who else is coming to the party?"

"No one. Lissa has, well, difficulty making friends."

A shudder of déjà vu slithered down her spine. "So did I when I was her age."

The thought seemed to cheer him. "Then there's hope for us after all."

"There's always hope." A wistful sadness tinged her

tone. C.J. was grateful the distraction of thumping feet in the next room kept him from noticing.

"Daddy, Daddy—" Lissa charged into the doorway, sweating with excitement. "Gramps and Gramma brought me so many presents! Come look!"

"Okay, punkin." Richard sucked a breath, cast a woeful glance over his shoulder and followed his happy child.

C.J. peeked under the kitchen table, where Rags had curled up with a dejected chin on his paws. "Don't touch the cake," she warned. "One whisker mark in that frosting, and your skateboard is history."

Rags whined.

"Just so we understand each other." She straightened, smoothed her own knit top, checked her makeup in the polished chrome of a nearby toaster, then pressed a clammy palm against her churning stomach, pasted a smile of welcome on her face and strode into the living room with a confidence she didn't feel. "Mr. and Mrs. McCade, how nice to see you again. My, aren't those gifts exquisitely wrapped. May I help you with them?"

She relieved a startled Sarah McCade of several items, carried them to the dining-room table where the other presents were stacked, while Thompson McCade's black stare burrowed tangibly into her back.

"What is she doing here?"

"I couldn't have a party without C.J.," Lissa chirped, oblivious to her grandfather's dark scowl. "She's my best friend in the whole wide world." The child scampered to the gift table, scanning it with huge eyes and a greedy grin. "Did you bring me a present, C.J.?"

Richard cleared his throat. "It's impolite to ask, Lissa."

She spun around, clearly surprised. "How come?"

"Ah, well, it just is."

C.J. chuckled, looped a loving arm around the girl's shoulders. "Guess you'll just have to wait until time to open them."

Lissa giggled and clapped. "Can I open them now?"

"Not now, punkin. You won't have anything to look forward to."

"Please, Daddy? I can't wait, I just can't."

Richard's indulgent smile wavered, and for a moment C.J. thought he'd give in.

Perhaps he would have, if Thompson hadn't stepped forward, glowering. "This is a family occasion."

"Now, dear—" Sarah touched her husband's arm, flinched when he pulled away, but this time the woman wasn't silenced by his disapproval. "This is Lissa's day. She's entitled to share it with whomever she chooses."

Still glaring at C.J., Thompson retrieved his pipe from his coat pocket, made a production of lighting it. "Let the child open her gifts," he said between puffs, then snapped the lighter shut without so much as a glance at Richard's angry face. "As Mother has pointed out, Lissa is entitled to do as she pleases."

"Yay!" Lissa spun around, grabbed an armful of colorful gifts and ran over to deposit them on the coffee table. "I'm gonna do this one first," she announced to her grandfather, who'd seated himself in his favorite lounge with a triumphant gleam in his eye. Sarah lowered her head, perched stiffly on an armless dining chair that had been placed in the modest conversation area to increase seating capacity.

Ignoring Richard, Thompson spoke directly to his

grandchild. "Open any of them you want, sweetheart. They're all for you."

Beaming, Lissa charged back for another armful while C.J. met Richard's gaze. They communed silently for a moment before she saw the resignation in his eyes. His smile was thin as he gestured to the sofa. "Come join us, C.J."

She would rather have eaten a lightbulb than move one step closer to Thompson McCade, but she did so anyway for Richard's sake. And for Lissa's.

She sat on the sofa, focusing a smile on poor Sarah McCade, who looked as if she wished the ground would heave up to swallow her whole. "It's nice to see you again," she told the woman, and was rewarded by a grateful smile. "That's a lovely suit. The color becomes you."

"It is nice, Sarah." Richard settled beside C.J., slipping a proprietary arm around her shoulders. "Is it new?"

Flushing, Sarah touched her mint-colored linen lapel. "Well, yes, actually." She might have said more, except that Lissa arrived with her final transport of packages.

After placing them reverently on the coffee table, the girl spun around, spotted C.J. and her father nested on one side of the sofa so close that a sheet of paper wouldn't fit between them. Lissa's smile wavered, went flat.

C.J. felt as if she'd suddenly swallowed a brick. She knew what was coming, and wasn't the least bit surprised when the child doggedly wedged herself between them. Richard, however, was clearly stunned, and might have spoken up if not for Thompson's approving chuckle.

Instead, Richard simply moved aside, allowing his daughter to squeeze between him and C.J. The child wiggled a finger at a small gift with a crooked, hand-tied bow. "That one first, Daddy."

Richard obligingly retrieved it. "This one is from me, punkin."

"I know." She grinned, squirmed with excitement. "Play the game now, please, play the birthday game."

Eyes warming, Richard smiled at his daughter's pleasure, held the gift above her head. "Heavy, heavy hangs over your head," he intoned. "What are you going to do with it?"

"Umm-m." She shifted, peered up at the package. "Play with it...no, wait!" Squenching her eyes, she amended the response. "Watch it!" She grabbed the present, ripped off the wrapping and squealed with excitement. "A Pinocchio tape! I knew it, I knew it, thank you, Daddy! I love it!" She hugged him fiercely, passed the tape around so all could admire it, then pointed to a package the size of a shirt box. "That one next!"

Richard laughed, retrieved the gift and held it over her head for the next round of the game. Lissa announced that she was going to wear its contents, only to discover that the present was a board game from her grandparents.

"You'll look pretty funny wearing *that* to school," Thompson teased.

Lissa giggled, everyone smiled, and for the next half hour tension disappeared as the adults enjoyed the delight of a child each of them loved. Even C.J. relaxed, completely swept up in the excitement of the moment, the joy of sharing Lissa's special day. She admired each gift, even laughed at Thompson's jokes and was rewarded by the cessation of hostile stares from the older man, who watched his beloved granddaughter with shining eyes, and blatant love.

"This is from C.J.," Richard announced, holding the shoe-box-shaped box above Lissa's head. He winked at C.J., intoned the proper mantra and handed over the package after Lissa determined that she was going to eat whatever was in the box.

C.J. snickered. "Goodness, I should have brought the ketchup."

Lissa glanced up from her ripping chores. "It's candy, isn't it? A whole big bag of those yummy lemon drops, like the ones you bought me when we went to the zoo."

"Open it and find out." C.J. exchanged a covert smile with Richard, who could barely contain his own excitement. "But somehow I think you'll have trouble washing this down with soda pop."

Intrigued, Lissa removed the remaining paper in two frenzied sweeps of her hand, yanked open the box and stared inside with her jaw gaping. "What am I supposed to do with them?"

"What do you think, silly goose?" C.J. reached in to remove the white satin ballet slippers. "You're supposed to wear them to ballet class."

"Daddy won't let me take ballet. He's afraid I'll get all sweaty and have an attack or something."

C.J. angled a glance over the little pigtailed head to smile at the child's grinning father. "Well, maybe your daddy changed his mind."

Hope leapt into Lissa's widening eyes. She spun on the sofa. "Daddy?"

It didn't seem possible for Richard to widen his grin,

but he did. "I just couldn't resist the image of my precious, pigtailed girl in a tutu."

Thompson lurched forward, eyes flashing with fury, jaw slackened in disbelief. "You can't be serious." He shook off his wife's restraining touch. "I won't allow it."

C.J. slipped an arm around Lissa's shoulders as if the ineffectual gesture could protect the quivering child from the battle both feared was imminent.

To his credit, Richard simply smiled coolly, spoke with soft determination that brooked no argument. "The decision is mine, Thompson. After consultation with both Lissa's physician and respiratory therapist, C.J. has developed a program that will allow Lissa to safely participate."

C.J. flinched as McCade glowered at her. "You. I should have known."

Before either Richard or C.J. could respond, Lissa wriggled forward. "Please, Gramps, I want to take ballet, I really, really want to."

A vein bulged at Thompson's hairline. His gaze darted from C.J. to Lissa, softened only slightly. He leaned back, clamped the pipe stem between his teeth and spoke from the corner of his mouth. "I see."

Sarah, perched so stiffly on the edge of her chair that her rigid back resembled a linen-clad ruler, tried desperately to appease both sides. "I'm certain Ms. Moray will take every precaution to ensure Lissa's lessons are both safe and enjoyable."

Recognizing the woman's desperate plea, C.J. provided the reassurance she clearly sought. "Please rest assured that Lissa's health is paramount, and will be closely monitored—''

Thompson interrupted gruffly. ''Mother, bring Lissa's big gift.''

Richard frowned. Lissa beamed.

Sarah rose from the chair, nervously rubbing her hands. ''Yes, of course, dear.'' The poor woman angled what appeared to be an apologetic glance at C.J. before hurrying out the front door.

''There's more presents?'' Lissa asked through her happy grin.

''Just one.'' Thompson deliberately paused to retrieve his lighter, then angled a gloating glance at his clearly perplexed son-in-law. ''But it's very special.''

''Wow.'' Eyes gleaming, Lissa returned the ballet slippers to their box and laid it aside, freeing her lap for more loot just as Sarah McCade reentered the room carrying a large, flat item the size of a small card table.

Sporting a befuddled frown, Richard instantly leapt up to assist the struggling woman. ''I, ah, think you'll have to come open it here,'' he told Lissa. ''It's much too large to hold over your head.''

The child was off the sofa before her father had finished verbalizing the suggestion. ''Wow, it's so *big!*'' Without waiting for the birthday mantra, she uttered an excited squeak and tore at the wrapping until the carpet was littered with ribbons and ripped paper.

When the gift was revealed, Lissa stood back with a stunned stare. A painted replica of herself stared back, along with the dark-eyed smile of a woman C.J. recognized from a framed photograph on the lamp table.

''That's my mom,'' Lissa whispered, clearly confused

to see an image of herself at her present age embraced by a woman who'd died when she was barely two. The artist had clearly superimposed images from separate photographs to create a commissioned oil painting of nine-year-old Lissa in the arms of the mother she could barely remember.

After a final puff on his pipe, Thompson propped an ankle on his knee, leaned back with a gloating grin. "Your mother will always be with you, my dear. Never forget that."

C.J. felt as if she'd been gut-punched. The reminder was not meant only for Lissa. Everyone in the room knew it.

Rags chased the ball across the backyard, disappearing into the lengthening twilight shadows. A moment later, he returned, tail swishing, to drop the soggy tennis ball at C.J.'s feet. She retrieved it gingerly. Behind her, the back door opened. C.J. moistened her lips, took a bracing breath and tossed the ball again.

"Is Lissa asleep?" she asked as the dog bounded happily after the toy.

The door closed. "Yes." Richard moved beside her, hesitating before slipping an arm around her shoulders. "I'm sorry for what happened."

"It wasn't your fault." As Rags tore back across the yard to drop the ball at her feet, C.J. absently retrieved it. "Was Lissa upset?"

"Confused. She doesn't understand what's going on."

"I don't, either." Alerted by Rags's impatient bark, C.J. tossed the ball, watched the joyful pooch scamper after it. "I take that back. Certainly the McCades can't be faulted for wanting to keep their daughter's memory alive. If I was in their position, I'd feel threatened by anything or anyone that appeared to devalue that memory, so I can see why Mr. McCade is less than thrilled by my intrusion into his granddaughter's life. What I don't understand is why he's so hostile to you, the father of his only grandchild. It's almost as if he blames you for—'' C.J. bit her tongue, horrified by what had almost slipped out of her mouth. She angled a glance at Richard, saw the stiff rigor of his jaw, the hard glint in his eye. ''I'm sorry. I had no right—''

''There's no 'almost' about it. Thompson does hold me responsible for Melinda's death. He always has. He always will.''

Flinching at his harsh tone, C.J. turned away from the excited animal scampering toward her with the fuzzy green ball in his mouth, a signal that the game had ended. From the corner of her eye, she saw Rags drop the ball, then wander off with his tail drooping. She touched Richard's shoulder, whispered a single word. ''Why?''

His eyes closed, as if he'd been expecting the question, yet dreaded it nonetheless. ''Because I am responsible.''

Whatever C.J. had expected to hear, that was not it. Her hand sprang away as if singed, and she stumbled back a step.

Richard heaved an unhappy sigh, rubbed his eyelids. ''Melinda was a fragile person, both physically and emotionally. I knew that from the moment I met her, but I didn't care. I loved her.'' He shuddered, lowered his hand to rest a loose fist against his chin. ''I wanted to protect her, to make her feel secure. She was used to nice things, so I surrounded her with them, then I dashed to the office, put in twelve-hour days to pay for them. I told myself I was doing it for her, but I was doing it for me, because I was ambitious, because I wanted to succeed.''

''There's nothing wrong with ambition.''

''There is when it destroys the people you love.'' He turned away, but not before she saw the misery in his eyes. ''It won't surprise you to know that Thompson was staunchly against my marriage to his daughter. Melinda adored her father, spent her entire life trying to please a man for whom no effort was ever quite good enough. She married me anyway, although I never figured out whether it was an act of rebellion against her father, or a futile attempt to gain peace between the two most important men in her life.''

''A clash between husband and father isn't unique,'' C.J. said quietly. ''My father despised my older sister's fiancé. I think he felt, well, abandoned, as if he truly was losing a daughter. My sister married anyway, and eventually, my father accepted her husband. It was a slow process, and not an easy one, but eventually they were able to establish a workable relationship. Not that my family's situation is anything like yours, of course. I mean, it might be, but—'' C.J. huffed a breath, extended a hand. ''For heaven's sake, say something, do something to shut me up. I'm making a terrible mess out of this.''

To her surprise, he smiled, lifted her hand to his lips. ''You're just trying to help.''

''But I'm not helping, am I?''

The sadness crept back into his eyes. ''No one can help.''

C.J. still didn't understand, and said so.

Richard shrugged, turned to lean against a pergola fragrant with climbing wisteria. "I didn't give Melinda the emotional support she needed because I was trying to prove myself worthy, not to my wife, but to her father. It became a battle of wills, a chess game with human pieces. Move, countermove, point, counterpoint. Everyone on the board was shoved from square to square without compassion or conscience. Melinda became a helpless pawn, forced to choose between two men who supposedly loved her, but who loved their own power more. We both knew she was distraught by our competition. We didn't care. Each of us was determined to win." He paused, studied a snowy wisteria blossom as if universal secrets were revealed within its fragrant folds. "After Lissa's birth, Melinda unraveled before my eyes. She couldn't deal with the emotional trauma of caring for a sickly child, and felt guilty, I think, as if our daughter's illness was caused by some personal failure on her part. By the time I pulled my head out of my ambition long enough to realize what was happening, it was too late. She'd already found another lover. This one came in a bottle."

The gasp C.J. heard came from her own lips.

"Shocked?"

"No, of course not. I mean…" She sighed, faced him. "Yes, I guess I am."

Richard's smile was wry, and sad. "So was I. So shocked I refused to recognize what was happening until I came home early and caught her sipping gin out of a coffee mug while our daughter sobbed in the playpen."

It cost C.J. to keep an impassive expression. Her stomach cramped, her lungs seemed to collapse on themselves. She inhaled slowly, chose her words with care. "You must have been terribly upset."

Richard's gaze wavered, his tongue darted to moisten his lips. He looked away before answering. "We fought that night. I hurled indignant accusations. She cried, pleaded for understanding. I, of course, was not in the mood to give it. I took Lissa into the nursery, and was changing her clothes when I heard our car squeal out of the driveway." He paused, swallowed hard. "The phone rang thirty minutes later. I knew without answering it that my wife was dead."

The power of his quiet voice nearly knocked C.J. over. She steadied herself on the patio table, shook her head as if denying reality. She wanted to speak, to offer condolence, but the words wouldn't come. There was nothing she could say to alleviate the haunting guilt of a tragedy that was not his fault, but for which he would always feel responsible.

"Witnesses said that she'd been driving erratically for miles before the car sideswiped a guardrail and flipped into the ditch." Richard gazed at the rising moon, slid a hand into his pocket. "I should have stopped her."

"You couldn't have stopped her, Richard." The words emerged choked, stilted. "Even if you'd had access to another car, you couldn't have left your baby alone."

A dull shrug, a lifeless voice. "I should have stopped her" was all he said.

So C.J. silently slipped her arms around the man she loved, laid her head against his weary shoulder and shed silent tears for a man too stoic to weep for himself.

Chapter Eight

"Jeté, jeté, plié, jeté. Isn't that neat, Daddy?" Flushed with excitement, Lissa pirouetted around the living room with her arms extended, fingertips touching as if she was hugging an invisible beach ball. "C.J. says I'm the best ballerina in the whole wide world."

"After two lessons?"

"Well, she says I could be the best if I really try hard, and there's this girl named Suzie in my class, and she likes me a whole lot, and she said I can come over to her house and practice sometimes." Lissa attempted an awkward arabesque, tilted into the sofa and stumbled forward, panting. "I'm gonna practice every single day until I can jump as high as C.J. can. Ballet is so fun, Daddy. I really, really love it."

"I'm glad, punkin. Just be careful you don't get too tired, okay?" Richard cupped his daughter's head, planted a kiss on her moist forehead. "Run in and change clothes now. Dinner will be ready in a few minutes."

"Okay." She gazed past her father's shoulder. "Are you staying for dinner, Gramps? We're having hamburgers."

Thompson McCade removed his unlit pipe from his mouth to balance the carved wooden bowl in his palm. "Not tonight, sweetheart." The girl acknowledged it without comment. After she'd scampered away, McCade fixed his son-in-law with a hard stare. "Where's the portrait?"

"In Lissa's room," Richard replied blandly. "It was a gift for her, was it not?"

The older man's mouth flattened. "I presumed Melinda's portrait would be displayed in a place of honor."

"It's hanging above her child's bed," Richard shot back. "Melinda would consider that the most honorable place in the house."

An angry flush crawled up McCade's throat. "It's that woman, isn't it? She's the reason you've lost respect for your wife, and are risking your daughter's life."

"I'm not going to dignify that with a reply."

As Richard turned away, McCade grabbed his shoulder, spun him around. "I won't tolerate this, Richard. You have no right to besmirch my daughter's memory with tawdry behavior. There are laws to protect children from lewd conduct in their presence."

"Lewd conduct?" Richard shook off McCade's hand, gaped in disbelief. "Are you out of your mind?"

"On the contrary, Richard. If you honestly believe I shall step aside and allow you to continue flaunting this unseemly affair in front of my grandchild, it is your mental acumen in question, not mine."

"Are you threatening me, McCade?" Balling his fists

at his side, Richard met his father-in-law's angry stare with one of cold fury. "Because if you are, if you make even the slightest effort to sully Ms. Moray's reputation, I'll personally jam that pipe so far down your throat that you'll be sitting on a lump for the rest of your miserable life."

"How dare you use that tone with me?"

"And how dare you insult the woman I'm going to marry?"

McCade stumbled as if struck, and in the stunned mirror of the old man's eyes Richard saw his own shocked reflection. The words had tumbled out unbidden, without conscious thought.

Of course Richard had considered remarriage, but always in the context of future possibilities. Having heard himself utter the commitment aloud was as much a shock to his own system as it was to his horrified father-in-law.

Ashen and clearly shaken, McCade swayed on his feet, touched his forehead as if feeling faint. "You can't be serious."

"I've never been more serious in my life." A euphoric sensation washed away anger and confusion, leaving Richard jubilantly buoyant, as if he could float with clouds. "C.J. is a wonderful woman. She's good for Lissa. She's good for me. I want us to be a family, and if she'll have me, we will be."

A glimmer of hope lit McCade's otherwise dead eyes. "So Ms. Moray has not yet agreed to this, er, ambitious plan of yours?"

Richard's optimism dissipated like a popped balloon. "She will," he replied with considerably more confidence than he felt, and would have added more emphasis had his father-in-law's gaze not fixated on a point beyond Richard's shoulder. He turned, felt as if he'd swallowed a brick.

Lissa stood in the hallway door, eyes huge, mouth quivering. "No!" she shouted. "You can't, Daddy, you just can't! I won't let you!" With a choked sob, the child sprinted down the hall and slammed her bedroom door.

"A brilliant child." Visibly delighted by his granddaughter's reaction, McCade rocked back on his heels and clamped the cold pipe stem between his teeth. "Clearly, she takes after her mother."

"I don't know, Bobbi. There was just something eerie about the whole thing, as if that poor woman's spirit had risen from the grave or something."

Bobbi huffed a breath, shouldered the camera strap. "That's silly, Ceejz. It was only a painting. The old man is just trying to get your goat, that's all."

"But to use his grandchild's birthday to advance a personal agenda?" C.J. shook her head slowly. "I don't think so. Thompson McCade may be a tyrant, but he genuinely loves Lissa. I can't believe he'd deliberately do anything to harm her. He's frightened, that's all."

"Frightened of what?"

C.J. shrugged, tossed the magazine she'd been perusing onto a coffee table cluttered by film boxes, an undeterminable wad of fabric and crumpled remnants of the morning newspaper. "Frightened that his daughter's memory will fade away."

"Poppycock. The old geezer just doesn't want anyone to take her place, that's all. Better watch your back, Ceejz."

"What?" C.J. straightened, leaned forward. "Why?"

"From what you've told me, the old man is out to slay the competition. That's you, hon."

"Me? No, not me. Uh-uh, definitely not me." She shot to her feet, absently began gathering clutter in a frenetic cleaning frenzy. "I'm just a friend, that's all, just a friend."

Bobbi paused at the front door, cast a knowing look over her shoulder. "Tell it to your heart, Ceejz. I know you too well."

C.J. straightened, clutching the mass of newspapers and tiny torn film boxes to her bosom. No words were spoken. None were needed.

Across the room, Bobbi regarded her with wise eyes, and a touch of sadness. "Don't do it again, hon, not this time."

Anxiety tightened her spine. "I don't know what you're talking about."

"The fellow with the polished chrome chopper, for one."

She managed a limp shrug. "Nice motorcycle."

"Nice guy," Bobbi shot back, "but you broke it off with him the minute he took you to meet his momma."

"He was looking for a serious relationship."

"And the rock-climbing hunk from Idaho?"

"He wanted a mom for his kids."

"What about the sharp dresser who raised blood-hounds for rescue work?"

Frustrated, C.J. jammed the silky fabric, which she vaguely recognized as one of Bobbi's favorite beach tops, into her armful of clutter and vengefully shoved the whole mess into the trash. "He wanted a commitment, dammit. I wasn't ready to lock the cage door on my life the way—'' C.J. bit off the words with a sharp breath. It was too late.

Bobbi finished the sentence for her. "The way your mother did?"

Too frightening to accept, too accurate to defend. "Look, I don't have to explain my love life, or lack thereof, to you or anyone else."

"Nope, you sure don't, but let's just have a quick review anyway."

"Aren't you late for work?"

Ignoring her roommate's grumpy glare, Bobbi issued a blithe shrug. "Since you've already discarded serious relationship, mother for kid, and commitment, exactly how do Richard and Lissa fit into your future?"

The unexpected question stunned her. "Future?"

"Yes, future, roughly defined as whatever time we have left before worms eat our eyes out." Impatiently shifting her camera and work valise, Bobbi narrowed her gaze. "Tell me, why are you always prodding me to marry Maury?"

Further rattled by the abrupt topic switch, C.J. found herself stammering. "Well, uh, b-because he's a good man, and you make each other happy."

"Exactly."

A slow heat warmed her cheeks. "It's not the same, and you know it."

"Do I? Richard is a good man, too. He makes you happy."

"Bobbi, please, you don't—"

"And unless I'm very much mistaken, Richard Matthews is a man looking for commitment, a serious relationship and a mother for his child, all of which have sent you screaming into the night on more than one occasion. So why, one might ask, are you still hanging around?''

Before C.J. could open her mouth, Bobbi was answering her own question. ''I'll tell you why. Because for the first time in that crazy, adventurous, whirlwind existence you call a life, you've actually fallen in love. Real, honest-to-goodness, head-over-heels, heart-pounding, can't-breathe, can't-think, can't-survive-another-minute-without-seeing-him, l-o-v-e love, and even though the very notion scares the liver out of you, you can't remember what your life used to be like before Richard was a part of it.'' A quick pause, a noisy gulp of air, and quick shriek elicited by her flickered glance at the wall clock. ''Oh, God! I'm late!'' She spun around, yanked open the door, charged out hollering, ''There are fresh cookies on the counter for your afternoon class. Don't forget to bring back the container.'' The door slammed.

Suddenly C.J. was alone. Alone with her thoughts. Alone with her fears. Alone with the gnawing terror that her roommate had been right about everything. Commitment. Serious relationship. Parenthood. Future.

Love.

All her life C.J. had feared love. Or rather, she'd feared the martyred existence she'd been taught love required. It had been tricky, treading that rainbow road of romance for a short distance, only to leap off before the love trap sprang. This time she'd missed the detour, had barely noticed when the cage clanged shut behind her.

She was caught, and yes, she was frightened, frightened by the swollen ache of her heart, the profundity of emotion, by the undeniable urge to look beyond the here and now into the vast vortex of the days and years to come. The future.

There had been times in her life when her illness had gotten the better of her, and C.J. had wondered if she even had a future. That's when she'd taught herself to focus on the moment, to survive just one more minute, one more hour, one more day. Tomorrow, she'd learned, would take care of itself.

In retrospect, she realized that long after her physical crisis passed she'd continued to control her future the same way she'd controlled every other aspect of her life, moment by moment, breath by breath, closing her eyes to anything beyond the sphere of the immediate.

Now everything had changed. All her tomorrows were spread out bright and glorious, just waiting for her to claim them as her own. Richard and Lissa could be a part of those tomorrows. They could be a part of her future, if only she could control her debilitating fear.

But even as C.J. silently vowed to try, her mother's martyred image flashed through her mind. The terror swallowed her whole.

"First position, backs straight, toes out, knees tight." C.J. paused to pat a bent little spine into ramrod stiffness, then moved down the line of bright-eyed beginners clutching the barre and casting admiring glances at themselves in the mirrored wall. "Arms up, reach high, reach for the sky, graceful fingers, girls, flowing, swaying, breezy fingers, like spring grass wafting in the wind...that's it, very good. Straight back, Jeanie, shoulders high...higher...that's great, wonderful." She clapped her hands. "Splendid, class, you're all doing beautifully. Practice toe positions, work on body line and I'll see you all on Monday afternoon."

The children whooped and swooped, spinning in a din of sudden chatter. They broke into small groups, one giggling cluster heading for a bench to remove their ballet slippers while a larger group crowded the buffet table for refreshments. Lissa, clad in neon pink tights and a swishy orange swing skirt, crouched at the barre with Suzie, who was several years older than Lissa, although she'd joined the beginner's class only a few weeks earlier. The two girls hunched together, whispering madly.

C.J. smiled, pleased that Lissa was enjoying herself, and even more pleased that the child had found a new friend. She absently retrieved a liter water bottle and towel from a nearby table, calling over her shoulder, "There's a special treat today, class. Bobbi's been baking cookies again."

More whoops, shouts of "yay!" as most of the remaining children sprinted toward the sugary repast.

C.J. had just finished drying her face and draping the towel around her neck when Suzie scooted over, eyes shining, face glowing with exertion and pride. "Did you see how good I did today, C.J.?"

"Yes, I did, sweetie. You've been practicing, haven't you?"

The metallic glint from a mouthful of silvery braces lit Suzie's happy grin. "My daddy put a ballet barre in my bedroom and a big long mirror, so I can practice all the time!"

"That's wonderful—" C.J. stumbled back a step as Lissa pushed herself in between them.

"I did good, too," she announced in a tone that brooked no argument. When a startled C.J. agreed that she had indeed done very well, Lissa issued a satisfied grunt, then angled a perturbed glance at her friend. "The cookies are almost gone."

Suzie's eyes widened in horror as she spun and scampered off to the refreshment table.

Immediately Lissa cocked her head, stared up at C.J. with nerve-racking intensity. "My back was real straight."

"Yes, it was."

"And I kept my toes real pointy, too."

"I noticed." C.J. also noticed the hint of a pout tugging the child's lower lip. Clearly Lissa was annoyed by not having been the center of attention during class, which wasn't unexpected, since it was a position she enjoyed in every other facet of her life. "You've done exceptionally well, Lissa, and I'm very, very proud of you."

The compliment pleased her, but only for a moment. Lissa pursed her lips, regarding C.J. with disturbing solemnity. "I did better than Suzie, didn't I?"

A wary tingle skittered across C.J.'s nape. "You both did very well."

"But you like me best, right?"

Something inside C.J.'s chest cracked. She crouched down to the child's level, brushed a damp wisp of brown hair away from pleading, heather gray eyes. "You are very, very special to me, Lissa." The girl's pupils widened in relief. "But it has to be our secret," C.J. added in a conspiratorial whisper. "We wouldn't want the other children to feel bad."

Lissa managed a somber nod. "Are you going to marry my daddy?"

C.J. clutched the girl's shoulders to keep herself from falling over. She rose slowly, cautiously. "Why on earth would you ask such a question?"

"Gramps said you only pretend to like me 'cause you want my daddy."

"Oh, honey." Because she couldn't help herself, she hugged the child fiercely. "That isn't true. I—"

"I brought you a cookie, Lissa," Suzie interrupted, happily oblivious. "It's the last one."

Lissa squirmed away, wiped her eyes with a balled fist. She sniffled, took the proffered cookie, eyed it with disappointment. "It's got chocolate in it."

"Uh-huh." Suzie took a bite of her own treat, chewing in ecstasy. "Chocolate chips are my very best favorite."

C.J. moistened her lips, forced an even tone. "Suzie, I wonder if you could excuse Lissa and me for a moment."

The girl appeared surprised by the request, but recovered with a nonchalant shrug and wandered back toward the juice bar. As soon as she was out of hearing range, C.J. turned to Lissa, who still clutched the cookie with tears in her eyes. "Sweetie, listen to me. You have to understand how much your daddy loves you. No one will ever take him away from you—"

The youngster's gaze moved past the cookie, which she promptly hid behind her back. "Hi."

A white warmth washed down C.J.'s spine. Richard's presence glided over her, through her, caressed her like a lover's touch. A familiar fragrance wafted past, spicy-sweet, musky and male. "Hi, punkin. How was class?"

"Okay."

His laugh rumbled straight into C.J.'s quivering heart. "Only 'okay'? Is this the same little girl who told me only this morning that she was going to be the 'bestest ballet dancer in the whole wide world'?"

With her hands still clasped behind her back, Lissa issued a limp shrug. "It was pretty okay, I guess." From the corner of her eye, C.J. saw Richard's eyes glaze briefly, but his smile never wavered. Lissa wobbled back a step. "I gotta get my stuff."

C.J. waited until the child crossed the room, then turned toward Richard. She wanted to tell him what Lissa had said, to warn him that she feared the child was feeling threatened by their relationship, but the moment her eyes met his her breath backed up in her throat and she could say nothing at all.

"You look beautiful," he whispered, reaching out to stroke a damp hair strand from her brow. "I never thought sweat was particularly sexy until I met you."

Dizzied by his touch, she moistened her lips, tried her voice again. "Men sweat. Women glow."

"So I've heard." He bent forward, and for a brief, shining moment, she thought he might kiss her. Instead, he whispered, "In your case, it's true. You are positively luminous."

Her lips twitched in disappointment even as her mind issued strong warning that with a dozen pair of curious little eyes watching their every move, kissing was definitely not a suitable option. Besides, C.J. was still rattled by her conversation with Lissa. "Richard, I have to talk to you."

"I have to talk to you, too."

"I'm quite concerned—" She finally caught the peculiar gleam in his eye. "About what?"

"It's Friday." He traced her jaw with his knuckle, allowed his fingertip to taste the corner of her mouth. "Lissa spends Friday nights with her grandparents, remember?"

"Oh." Her heart pounded with anticipation. "Right."

"I'll pick you up at seven. Unless that's too early…?"

"Ah, no. Seven is fine." A shaky breath cleared her mind. She'd speak with Richard about Lissa tonight, when there was more time. Together they could discuss the situation rationally, logically, and decide the best way to reassure a clearly frightened, insecure little girl.

Presuming, of course, that reassurance was even possible. When C.J. had been her age—

"Get a move on, punkin," Richard called out, interrupting her sad reminiscence. "Time's a-wasting."

Across the room Lissa finished stuffing her ballet slippers into her backpack, slipped the nylon strap over one shoulder before hurrying straight past C.J. and out the front door without so much as a backward glance.

Richard squeezed C.J.'s hand. "Tonight," he murmured.

A moment later he, too, was gone, and C.J. was thankfully swept up in the normal chaos of locating lost shoes, mopping spilled juice, waving goodbye to one class and greeting those arriving for the next.

The next two hours flew by in a pandemonium of music and laughter, of syncopated rhythms and twirling slippered feet. C.J. was immersed in her element, completely absorbed by the happy smiles of her students, and the joy of the dance.

Only later, after the final class had ended and the studio was dimly quiet, did C.J. recall the determination in Lissa's eyes as she'd strode from the room. Her expression had been chiseled, unmoving, more like a stone carving than a living child. It was eerily familiar, a ghost from her own haunted past, a translucent and spectral memory she couldn't quite identify, but which was nonetheless disturbing.

She tried to concentrate, to clarify the image, but suddenly her mind was filled by only one image, one thought, one memory. Richard. The shimmer of a gaze that caressed more erotically than a touch, the playful twitch of a smile so sensual the mere memory melted her bones like ice cubes in the sun, the image of primitive muscle rippling beneath civilized silk that made her palms itch with longing.

Richard. Smooth, sensual, sophisticated. Clumsy, cautious, comical. Gentle strength, stoic fear, a man both brash and courtly, who slipped into the spontaneous and whimsical or the calculating and deliberate with equal ease. He was a dichotomy, a man of many skins, wearing each with style if not comfort. He was unique. He was precious. He was everything C.J. admired, everything she feared.

She intuitively realized that tonight would be special. She didn't realize that it would also alter the entire course of her life.

Even in candlelight, the glitter of cut crystal was blinding. Shimmering chandeliers glimmered like a thousand dripping diamonds from an ornately carved ceiling so breathtakingly beautiful that it seemed more appropriate for an embassy drawing room than an exclusive French restaurant.

Beside her, Richard cupped a proprietary hand to her bare elbow, leaned to whisper. "You look magnificent. Even the maître d' can't take his eyes off you."

"He's just wondering why it's taking half the evening for us to follow him to a table." As she spoke, the starched fellow in question, who was hovering by a secluded table sparkling with crystal and gilded china, shot them another pained look.

Undaunted, Richard continued to guide her through the glistening ambiance at a leisurely stroll. "He'll be well rewarded for his patience. I want everyone here to get a good look at the most beautiful woman on earth."

She flushed at the praise, gave silent thanks that she'd worn the elegant, floor-length black satin rather than her personal favorite, a swingy red chiffon number that screamed "let's party," from its flirty peek of revealed cleavage to the flip of its swishy, thigh-high hem. The contrast with Richard's sleek, silk-trimmed dinner jacket would have been jarring, if not downright gaudy.

Eventually they reached their destination, were seated by the relieved maître d', who presented Richard with a wine list while two tuxedoed servers melted out of the walls to spread Irish linen across their laps and adjust padded tapestry footstools. Soft music floated through the room, delicate as the fragrance from a centerpiece of rose blossoms floating in a golden tureen of scented water.

C.J. was enraptured by the grandeur of it all. "This is the most magnificent place I've ever seen," she whispered when they were alone. "Do you come here often?"

A suave shrug settled into a boyish grin. "It's my first

time, but don't tell anyone. I'm trying to create an image here.''

''Ah, well, you're doing very nicely. I could have sworn you were an old hand at this.''

''I read a book.''

She laughed. ''Oh, right.''

''No, really.'' His earnest expression was offset by the absurd twinkle in his eye. *''How To Keep From Making a Fool of Yourself in Fancy French Restaurants.* Quite well written, actually, and there's an entire chapter on how to avoid ordering—how shall I put this?—entrees considered unique by the average American palate.''

A ladylike shudder was delicately suppressed. ''Would those avoidable entrees by any chance resemble, er, garden creatures?''

''Perhaps I shouldn't elaborate in case I misread the instructions.'' His smug smile tickled her immensely.

''All right,'' she warned with a chuckle. ''But if anything on my plate comes equipped with antennae or its own shell, neither one of us will be pleased by my reaction.''

''Understood,'' he replied, and would have said more if the maître d' hadn't chosen that moment to reappear with a silver ice bucket in which what appeared to be a large bottle of champagne was cooling.

Only when the cork was popped and C.J. caught a glimpse of the label did she realize that Richard had ordered a magnum of imported sparkling water, which the stone-faced maître d' served in fluted goblets, complete with raspberries and slices of lime.

Richard raised his glass for a toast. His fingers were trembling.

So were hers.

"To us," he murmured as crystal rims clinked.

Her heart hammered so loudly that she barely heard him. Suddenly she understood why he was so nervous, and why this night was so special.

Are you going to marry my daddy?

Lissa's question popped into her mind with such clarity that C.J. flinched.

Richard carefully set his glass aside. The contents sloshed anyway. A bead of moisture gathered along his upper lip. "Lissa told me what she said to you this afternoon."

C.J. felt faint. "Did she?"

"Yes." A thin smile. He absently touched his collar, as if wishing to loosen it. "She wasn't supposed to say anything, but you know how children are."

"Yes." The room was spinning. "I know how they are."

"She was reluctant at first. I mean, it's a big step for any family." He grabbed his goblet, drank half of it in a single swallow, then twirled the frosty stem between his palms. "But Lissa and I have discussed it, and we decided—that is, I decided, and she agreed—" He coughed, finished his drink and poured another. "Is it hot in here?"

"Stifling." She would have reached for her own glass if she could have focused on it.

Suddenly Richard reached out and snatched her hand with all the finesse of a wide receiver diving down a muddy field. "C.J., I know I'm no bargain, but you could do worse."

She blinked stupidly. "Worse than what?"

"Worse than me. I mean, I make a good living, I'm

kind to small animals, I keep in shape by jogging and I promise not to rebuild clocks on the dining-room table anymore.''

"Clocks.''

"If they make you crazy, I'll get rid of them.''

"Get rid of them?'' C.J. felt like a stoned parrot, but was powerless to control a mind so muddled she feared that she'd been sucked into some kind of wild, surrealistic dream.

Across the table, Richard's handsome face was tight with tension. "All that boinging and bonging every hour. It makes me crazy, too. I'll toss them all out, every last one of them, just say yes, C.J.'' He took a shuddering breath, squeezed her hand so tightly it went numb. "I want to marry you, C.J. I want you to be my wife.''

"Marry you.'' The words bounced balloonlike through her fuzzy brain. "Marry—'' her mind cleared slowly, joyfully "—you.''

"You'd make me the happiest man on—''

"*Pardonnez-moi*, Monsieur Matthews.'' The maître d' laid a cordless telephone beside Richard's plate. "Please forgive the intrusion. I am told it's a matter of some urgency.'' With an apologetic bow, the man slipped discreetly into the shadows.

A bewildered frown puckered Richard's brow as he brought the phone to his ear. "Yes?'' The frown flattened, his eyes clouded. "When...where...? Yes, yes, of course.'' He laid the phone aside, gazed across the table with a shattered expression more revealing than words.

C.J. knew instantly that something had happened to Lissa. Something terrible.

Chapter Nine

It would normally be a twenty-minute drive from the restaurant to the hospital. Richard made it in ten.

In a frantic swirl of satin and silk, they rushed through the lobby into the emergency waiting room where Thompson McCade paced frantically. His wife sat ramrod straight on a vinyl armchair, her handsome, aging face stoic and colorless.

The hospital surrounded Richard like a shroud, the stinging scent of antiseptic, the sterile drone of professional voices wafting beyond the cramped, parlor-style waiting area, hushed voices of personnel discussing life-and-death issues with the same matter-of-fact inflection that one used ordering pizza. It was terrifying, repulsive. All too familiar.

"Where is she? Where's my daughter?" Richard's first question was issued to McCade, the second to a uniformed attendant visible through an open pass-through window. A massive filing cabinet jammed with patient charts blocked any view of the medical unit itself, although a scant peek of an empty bed partially concealed by a teal green privacy curtain was available to those who, like Richard, were audacious enough to shove a head through the open window.

Startled by the intrusion, the attendant composed himself quickly, cast a covert glance down at the desktop and a questionnaire completed in Sarah McCade's distinctive handwriting. "Mr. Matthews?" At Richard's affirmative nod, the pleasant-faced young man issued a reassuring smile. "The doctor will speak to you in a moment."

"Is Lissa all right? Can I see her? I'm her father, dammit!" Frantic when the attendant issued an apologetic shrug and walked away, Richard spun on his ashen-faced father-in-law. "What in hell happened?"

"What do you think?" McCade snapped. "While you were out gallivanting, your daughter had another attack." His gaze swept past Richard, to the trembling woman beside him. "What's she doing here?"

To her credit, C.J. ignored the vitriolic question, seated herself beside Sarah. She took the older woman's hand, spoke in a voice hushed with compassion. "Is there something I can get for you?"

Sarah's smile was brave and grateful. "No, thank you, dear. We've been through this before. Lissa will be fine, just fine. The doctors will fix her right up. They always do...." The final assurance lost steam as Sarah bit her lip, focused a moist gaze somewhere in space. "Father went into his study after dinner," she murmured. "Lissa went to watch television. Her favorite show was on, the one where that cute little dog dresses up in period costume. I'd promised to watch it with her as soon as I cleared the dishes. It only took a few minutes, but by the time I joined her, she was gasping, almost blue. Her eyes had rolled back and her face was so swollen—'' Voice breaking, she lowered her gaze, fumbled in her purse for a tissue. ''She's never been this bad before. I shouldn't have left her alone.''

''It wasn't your fault.'' C.J. looked as if she wanted to say more, but was cut off when the emergency-room door opened. A white-coated physician emerged clutching a hinged, steel-clad chart and wearing a concerned frown.

Richard practically dived on him. ''My daughter...can I see her?''

''Not at the moment. She's still in some respiratory distress.'' The young doctor frowned at scrawled chart notes. ''In addition to her asthmatic condition, there is severe esophageal swelling symptomatic of allergic reaction. It would be helpful to know what we were dealing with here. Has she recently come in contact with any known allergens, or perhaps consumed something beyond her normal diet which may have precipitated such response?''

Stunned, Richard stepped back, cast questioning glances first at McCade, then at Sarah, who lifted a helpless hand.

''I served broiled chicken, and mashed potatoes. No gravy, of course. Father must watch his fat intake.'' The poor woman's eyes were pools of abject misery. ''Green beans, I think...yes, green beans and biscuits, and apple pie for dessert.''

The physician flipped through the chart pages, of which there were dozens. Lissa had been here before.

Many times, Richard thought sadly. Too damned many times.

"Has your daughter shown adverse reaction to any of those foods in the past?"

Richard was at a loss. "No, none."

"Had she taken any medications, cold remedies, analgesics, cough drops?"

"No," Richard replied after MaCade confirmed that she hadn't.

"Could she have come in contact with cosmetics, ointments, cleaning solutions or any other—"

"Chocolate." C.J.'s whisper reverberated through the small room like a bomb. She stood slowly, her skirt vibrating as if her knees trembled beneath black satin. Every trace of color had drained from her face. "It was chocolate."

If C.J. was pale as death, McCade was purple with outrage. "That's ludicrous," he boomed. "Do you honestly believe we'd have any substance in our house that makes our granddaughter violently ill?"

The doctor snapped the chart shut, focused on C.J. "Chocolate? Are you certain?"

"Yes," she replied miserably. "I'm certain."

Richard was vaguely aware of a raucous buzz. The emergency-room door lock clicked open, and the doctor disappeared back into the bowels of the medical unit, leaving the traumatized family members to deal with their shock, and their suspicion.

Touching her lips, C.J. took a shaky breath, met Richard's incredulous gaze with one of sheer misery. "I brought chocolate chip cookies to class today. Lissa was given one. I naturally assumed that she'd returned it—"

"You!" McCade stormed over, shook his finger in C.J.'s face. "You did this. I should have known. You've caused nothing but trouble for this family. Are you happy now, or will you only be satisfied when you've destroyed us all?"

C.J. vibrated as if struck, but made no attempt to defend herself as McCade continued to spew his rage. Richard was too stunned to react. His mind had completely disassociated from what was happening. Nothing made sense, nothing seemed real.

It was Sarah who ended her husband's tirade, grabbing his arm and spinning the big man around with surprising force. "That's enough," she snapped, her eyes flashing with a fire Richard had never seen the normally timid woman display. "None of this is C.J.'s fault, and I will not allow you to terrorize her the way you terrorized our poor daughter."

McCade's purple rage dissipated like so much steam. His jaw slackened, jowls drooping, eyes reflecting astonishment and disbelief. "How dare you say such a thing?"

"Because it's true," Sarah replied quietly. "And because if I'd spoken up years ago, Melinda might still be alive."

Other than C.J.'s hushed gasp, the room was silent as a tomb. From Richard's vantage point, he saw McCade's eyes glaze, his lips part in soundless protest. For a moment, he almost felt sorry for the man.

Stepping back, McCade slumped, slipped an agonized glance over his shoulder. "I loved my daughter. She was my life."

Hesitantly, Sarah went to her husband and laid a gentle hand on his shoulder. "I know that, dear, but I fear that

Melinda didn't. How could she? You were so strict with her. No matter what she did, what she accomplished, it was never right, never good enough. Year after year, I saw what was happening, watched her spirit shrink before my eyes, and I did nothing to protect her. If I had, perhaps she wouldn't have felt compelled to marry the first man who was kind to her." The moment the words were out of her mouth, Sarah gasped, spun to face Richard, her eyes wide with horror. "Oh, dear, I didn't mean... That is, I'm certain Melinda loved you deeply—"

"It's all right, Sarah. I understand." The worst part was that he truly *did* understand. His mother-in-law had simply verified what Richard had suspected all along, that in her desperation to escape one unhappy life, his wife had found herself unwittingly ensconced in another.

Suspecting was one thing. Knowing was another. It hurt.

Without speaking, C.J. crossed the small room, touched Richard's hand. He couldn't look at her. What must she think of him, a man so blind, so desperate that he'd taken a wife who had never loved him? A gentle pressure on his wrist answered, as if saying it didn't matter.

But it did matter. It mattered to Richard.

McCade turned his back to the room. Sarah sadly returned to her seat, sat stiffly, primly, with her hands crossed in her lap and her clouded gaze fixed somewhere in the past. The air was heavy with tension, with secrets revealed and those still unspoken, with silent recrimination and quiet fear and bleak despair of a family shattered, perhaps beyond repair.

Minutes ticked by. No one spoke, no one moved. Inside the open window, the attendant went about his routine, answering phones, shuffling papers, then moving out of sight again.

Time became the enemy. Time to reflect, to consider the impact of truths unburied, and the effect on a future that was now very much in doubt. Richard had known about Melinda's strained relationship with her father, but hadn't really understood it. If he had, he would have realized that Thompson McCade's excessive leniency and indulgence of his grandchild was a frantic attempt to right the wrongs visited on his own daughter.

The correction had been extreme, of course. Richard should have stepped in more forcefully, more often. Now he realized that he'd been hesitant to do so because on some level he'd understood McCade's desperation to make amends in the only way he knew how. So Richard had abdicated his parental responsibilities, allowing his own child to be spoiled as a ludicrous panacea for the tyranny of her mother's childhood.

Foolish. Dangerous. Perhaps even deadly.

If anything happened to Lissa, Richard didn't know how he could live with the pain. Or the guilt.

More minutes ticked by. Richard stood in the center of the waiting room, unmoving, unspeaking, oblivious to the passage of time. Reacting to a vague ache in his lower back, he shifted positions, realized that C.J. was no longer beside him. A quick glance around the room found her seated on a thin-cushioned sofa beside the open door leading to the lobby.

Her cheeks were pale enough to be worrisome, her eyes cloudy, almost dazed. Without noting that she was being observed, she fumbled with her sleek black dinner bag, retrieved a small disk he recognized as one of the glucose wafers she always carried.

A warning chill alerted him, but before he could absorb its implication the emergency-room door opened, and the white-coated attendant peered out. "Mr. Matthews, your daughter has responded well to treatment, and is feeling much better. You can see her now, if you'd like."

Richard nearly knocked the man over rushing through the door.

Twenty minutes later Richard returned to the waiting room feeling relieved, reflective and perennially perplexed, which was, he supposed, a normal condition of fatherhood. Children were confusing creatures, charmingly candid, spontaneously sincere, yet capable of evasion tactics intricate enough to garner a politician's envy.

Sarah set a magazine aside, rose to her feet. "How is she, dear?"

"A little groggy from the medication, but doing well. She'll be here a few days. They want to do some tests."

A strangely subdued Thompson McCade slouched in his chair, fiddling with his unlit pipe. He glanced up, looked quickly away, but not before Richard saw the sadness in his eyes. The older man spoke quietly, almost apologetically. "Are we allowed to see her?"

"They'll take her to her room soon. Then you can see her."

McCade nodded without making eye contact, said nothing more.

"Was she able to tell you what happened?" Sarah asked.

It wasn't a question Richard wanted to answer, nor was

he certain that he even could. Lissa had issued a few
mumbled replies, acknowledging that she'd hidden the
chocolate chip cookie in her backpack and eaten it after
supper. When Richard had asked why she'd done such a
thing when she knew it would make her sick, the child
had merely shrugged and fidgeted with the corner of the
blanket. In fact, she'd issued a limp shrug in reply to just
about every question Richard had posed.

Lissa herself had had only one question, and it had
been a strange one. She'd wanted to know if C.J. was
mad at Suzie for having given her the cookie. When
Richard replied that he doubted C.J. was angry with anyone, Lissa had seemed oddly disappointed, if not downright annoyed.

"Richard...dear?"

"Hmm?" He blinked, realized Sarah was speaking to
him. "Oh, well, it seems C.J. was right. Lissa sneaked a
cookie out of class."

Clearly shaken, Sarah lowered herself to the chair.
"That's so unlike Lissa."

"Yes, it is." Richard glanced around the waiting
room. "Where is C.J., anyway?"

"In the cafeteria, I believe." Sarah heaved an unhappy
sigh, furrowed a neatly penciled brow. "I don't think she
was feeling well."

The implication hit Richard like a fist. They'd left the
restaurant before she'd had so much as a bite of bread.
That had been hours ago. Before he'd gone in to see
Lissa, he'd noticed C.J.'s telltale pallor, the trembling of
her hands as she'd fumbled with the glucose supplement.
Obviously her blood sugar levels had dropped low
enough to precipitate a reaction.

"Richard, where are you going? Richard...?"

But he was already out the door and halfway across the hospital lobby.

The cafeteria was quiet, nearly empty except for a few scattered stragglers occupying a few of the molded plastic tables and chairs packed throughout the cavernous room. Hot food service had ceased hours earlier, but a wall of vending machines supplied drinks, snacks and a few dubious sandwiches.

C.J. washed a bite of one such sandwich down with a sip of unsweetened iced tea before pushing the dry remnants away. She nibbled a potato chip. Her stomach protested, but she paid it no mind. Having already injected a precise insulin dosage in anticipation of a large meal, C.J. realized that her body required a counted number of nutritional grams whether she was hungry or not.

Such was her life. She'd long since given up railing about the injustice of it all. Things were as they were, and one either accepted reality or spent a miserable existence locked in a lifelong pity party. Pity was definitely not C.J.'s style, not for herself, not from others.

As she wadded up the empty chip bag, she glanced across the room and saw a familiar figure hover in the doorway. He spotted her quickly, picked his way between scattered tables to join her.

Richard sat down, brows puckered, eyes earnest and filled with concern. "Are you all right?"

The question startled her. "Of course."

"I'm so sorry. I should have realized..." Whatever it was he should have realized remained a mystery as the words disappeared into a pained breath. "You must think me incredibly dense."

"Dense?" An absent shake of the head did little to clear her befuddlement. "What on earth are you talking about?"

Richard extended a hand, let it fall back onto the table.

A niggling doubt tightened C.J.'s stomach. "Lissa *is* all right, isn't she? I wouldn't have left the waiting room except that the attendant assured me she was doing well."

"Lissa's fine. She'll be home in a few days."

"A few days?"

"They want to do some tests and watch her for a while to make certain there aren't any residual effects. She had an extremely violent reaction." He fingered the wadded chip wrapper, avoiding her gaze. "You were, ah, right about the cookie."

C.J.'s stomach lurched, but she managed an impassive nod.

"How did you know?" he asked, bouncing the balled wrapper on his palm.

"Lucky guess." She hoped he would let it go at that.

For a moment, it seemed as if he would. He blandly studied the crinkled cellophane, then viciously crushed it inside his closed fist. "I don't understand why," he murmured. "She knew it would make her sick."

C.J. felt mildly ill. "Yes, she knew."

"Then why?" He slammed his fist on the table, startling the cafeteria's few patrons. "What was she thinking? Lissa is my daughter, my own flesh and blood, but sometimes I look at her, and I realize that we're practically strangers. I don't understand my own child. What kind of father does that make me?''

"It's not your fault, Richard. You can't understand what you've never experienced. No one expects you to."

"What I've never experienced?" A pathetic befuddlement furrowed his brow. "That doesn't make sense. I mean, I was a child once myself. Is the perspective of girls so much different than that of boys?''

The question was issued with such endearing earnestness that C.J. would normally have responded with a smile. But not now, not with ghosts of her own past circling like vultures. "Yes, actually, I suspect that boys and girls grow up with very different perspectives, but that's not what I meant."

Frowning, Richard dropped the crushed chip wrapper, steepled his hands beneath his chin. The wary glint in his eye gave her pause. "I'm listening."

To compose herself, C.J. took another sip of tea. Condensation dripped from the can, staining the bodice of her satin gown. She set the can aside, dabbed the moisture with a napkin. The ineffectual gesture gave her a focus point, an excuse to avoid the eyes of the man who would no doubt despise her when her secret was revealed.

She dabbed, studied the moist blotch, dabbed some more, and heard the sound of her own hushed and trembling voice. "Children who are sick," she was saying, "children who are different, live with the secret terror that they aren't worthy of being loved. It eats away at their spirit, splinters their self-esteem. Most of these children will eventually create situations to prove themselves wrong, to assure themselves that they truly are loved. Sometimes, the situations they create are dangerous.''

From the corner of her eye, she saw Richard's head vibrate, but he said nothing.

She crumpled the paper napkin, placed it on the table. "When I was a child, I was desperately jealous of my brothers and sisters. They went outside and played, ate anything they wanted, didn't have to stick themselves with needles twice a day. But most of all, they had our father's attention."

Tears pricked her eyes. She blinked them away, dived deep into the recesses of her mind to share the one secret she'd always kept hidden. Until now.

A deep breath, a determined gaze. "Every Sunday afternoon I'd watch from my bedroom window while my father and siblings played touch football on the front lawn. It was tradition, I suppose, but I resented it terribly. One Sunday, I asked my father to stay with me instead. I told him we could watch television, or play a board game, or do anything at all as long as we did it together." She moistened her lips, cast a pleading glance across the table. "I just wanted to spend time with him."

Richard's eyes softened sympathetically. "Of course you did."

Shivering, C.J. took a ragged breath, looked away. "Daddy was not pleased by the request, not pleased at all. He said I was being selfish, and pointed out that the other children were being neglected because my mother spent all her time taking care of me. He said my brothers and sisters deserved attention, too, and basically told me to stop behaving like a spoiled brat." She shrugged, dabbed the moisture from her eyes. "In retrospect, I realized he was right. I was spoiled and overindulged. My

illness assured that I was also the center of my parents'
attention. It just wasn't the kind of attention I wanted.''

Richard shifted, clearly surprised and discomfited by
her revelation. C.J. presumed his uneasiness sprang from
the obvious parallel between her own early experiences
and that of his daughter. ''It must have been difficult for
you,'' he murmured, studying the marred plastic tabletop.
''But surely you don't blame your parents for your illness? I mean, it must have been difficult for them, too.''

''Actually, I did blame them.''

Richard's head snapped up. ''What?''

''I was a child, Richard. A child.'' She tried for a
reassuring smile, but knew it did little to alleviate the
shock of her words. ''Children don't understand things
the way adults do. They gaze up with bright little eyes,
and nod their heads with astute vigor, but they truly don't
understand the logic, the rationale of what's being explained. All they know is that something bad has happened to them, and Mommy and Daddy won't make it
go away.''

Clearly aghast, Richard stammered, ''That's not real-
istic. Parents aren't gods.''

''They are to their children.'' C.J. touched his hand,
whispered softly, ''I know this isn't what you want to
hear, but this is how I felt when I was Lissa's age, and
unless I'm very much mistaken, it's the way she's feeling
right now. There's nothing you can do to change her
anger, irrational though it may be, but it's important that
you at least understand, give her permission to be angry,
allow her to own her emotions instead of feeling guilty
for having even experienced them. Illness is very confusing for a child, especially a covert, controlled illness

that prevents participation in normal activity even when the child is feeling perfectly fine.''

Richard rubbed his eyes, shook his head. ''This is incredible.''

''I know.''

He looked up, eyes frantic. ''What can I do?''

''Protect her.''

''From what?''

''From herself.'' C.J. glanced away, balled her hands in her lap. ''Perhaps I should finish my story.''

He leaned back in the chair, regarded her harshly. ''Yes, perhaps you should.''

C.J. flinched, swallowed. ''Anyway, my feelings were hurt. My father had called me selfish and manipulative, which of course I was, but that made me nonetheless determined to wreak revenge. I wanted him to be sorry he'd hurt me, sorry he'd said those things. I wanted to be the center of attention again, and I knew just how to do it.'' She angled a sideways glance, cringed at his flinty stare. ''Unfortunately, I miscalculated and ended up putting myself in a coma. I would have died if my brother hadn't found me on the bathroom floor mere minutes after I'd injected myself with what turned out to be a near-lethal dose of insulin.''

Richard's jaw twitched. He stared at C.J., then down at the table, studied his own tapping fingers. After a long moment, he spoke without looking up. ''You deliberately made yourself sick to punish your parents?''

A fresh batch of tears welled up without warning. ''Yes.''

''And you think my daughter did the same thing?''

''I think,'' she replied carefully, ''that Lissa is a very

angry, very confused little girl who does not want to share her daddy's love and attention.''

Only his eyes showed emotion, a flicker of anger, disbelief, profound sadness. "You're wrong."

C.J. didn't think so. She said nothing.

After a long moment, Richard pushed roughly away from the table, shot to his feet and stood there, raking his hair, rubbing his face with his palms. "Lissa is a very intelligent, very loving child. She wouldn't do such a thing." He skewered C.J. with a look. "Frankly, I don't understand how you could have done such a thing, either.''

Her heart sank to her toes. "I know."

"It was cruel."

"Yes."

"My God, your parents loved you. Can you imagine what you put them through? How could you be so heartless, C.J., how could you make them suffer like that?''

She clutched her stomach, stared down at her trembling lap without responding. There was no defense he would accept, no excuse that mattered. She understood his denial, his terror at even the hint that his daughter might have deliberately hurt herself as a manipulative ploy.

And C.J. also understood that Richard was lashing out at her because there was nowhere else he could lay his anger, and his fear.

"I love my daughter." He ground out the words through tightly clamped teeth. "Lissa knows that. She doesn't have to resort to medical theatrics to get my attention." He sucked a raspy breath. When he spoke again, his voice was soft, incredulous, trembling with leashed rage. "Did you by any chance share this same story with her?"

"Certainly not!" She snapped her head back to meet his accusing gaze with one of stark horror. "Are you suggesting that I actually gave her the idea?"

"Not deliberately, of course." His anger dissipated into pained perplexity. "It's just that you have spoken with her about your own childhood—"

C.J. shot to her feet. "Lissa felt alone, frightened. She needed to know that someone understood what she was going through, that she could live a happy, normal life in spite of her illness. She needed hope, Richard, and I gave it to her."

His expression crumpled before her eyes. "Oh, God. I'm sorry. Honey—" He took her arm, stopping her as she turned away. "Please forgive me. I didn't mean that, honest to God, I didn't. All you've ever done is try to help my daughter, and you have helped, more than you'll ever know. That's why you're good for her." He released her arm, softened his tone. "That's why you're good for me."

Their eyes met, and in the gentle depths of his gaze C.J. saw the secret of his soul laid bare before her. An anguished throb softened her heart, for she knew what he would say next, and she knew how she must respond.

Richard lifted her hand, stroked her knuckles with his thumb. "Lissa needs you in her life, C.J. I need you. Together we can become a real family." He licked his lips, managed a nervous smile. "Earlier this evening I asked you a question. You never had the chance to answer it. Will you, C.J., will you do me the honor of becoming my wife?"

Every drop of moisture evaporated from her mouth. Her hands chilled to the bone, her legs threatened to collapse like wet noodles. Each word formed meticulously in her mind, was forced from her lips with agonizing care. "What Lissa needs is her father. She adores you, Richard, and she doesn't want to share. I can't blame her for wanting your undivided attention, nor can I be responsible for what she might do in the future to assure herself that she has it. No——" She touched his lips, silencing his protest. "I know you don't believe that Lissa deliberately made herself ill tonight, but I do. She knew we would be together, and she knew you were going to propose marriage. Don't you see, Richard, she couldn't stand the thought of someone else being in your life? I can't marry you, Richard, and I think——" her voice cracked "——I think it's best that we not see each other again."

He released her hand, stepped back as if he'd been slapped. "You don't mean that."

"I do mean it, Richard." She had to mean it. "Goodbye." Mustering a strength she didn't believe she had, C.J. turned to leave, pausing only when Richard called her name. She hesitated, looked over her shoulder.

He stood where she'd left him, with one hand extended and heartbreak in his eyes. "I love you."

"I know," she whispered. Then, blinking back tears, she walked quietly out of his life.

Chapter Ten

"If your chin droops any lower, you're going to trip on it." Bobbi draped one chummy arm around her roommate's slouched shoulders, used her free hand to retrieve the portable telephone from a cluttered, scissor-legged metal tray that doubled as the apartment's communication center. "You've been moping around for nearly a week. C'mon, hon. Call him."

C.J. shook her head. "I can't."

"Sure you can. You just punch a few of these little buttons, and voilà! Richard answers. You talk, he talks, you hang up, he hangs up, then you both rush out, meet at a romantic hideaway and make love like bunnies." Bobbi grabbed C.J.'s hand, slapped the phone into it. "Trust me, hon. Maury and I are living proof that it works."

Heaving a pained sigh, C.J. replaced the telephone in its charger, paused to fidget with a chewed pencil protruding from a scattered pile of phone notes and a few of Bobbi's crumpled eyeglass-cleaning tissues.

"I appreciate your concern," C.J. said carefully. "But the situation between Richard and me is considerably different than your relationship with Maury. It has to be. Richard's primary responsibility is to his child, a child who is sick and frightened of losing the only parent she has left. They have enough grief in their lives. I won't create more."

"How are you going to do that?" Bobbi demanded, poking her slipping spectacles back into place. "By loving them both so much that you'd slice your own heart into sushi before you'd hurt either one of them? Get a grip, Ceejz. The man loves you, and you love him. Just pick up the danged phone and tell him so."

Pushing away, C.J. strode to the galley-style kitchen, yanked a liter of chilled water out of the fridge. She unscrewed the cap, took a healthy sip to compose herself. "Lissa could have died," she said finally.

"And probably would have, if you hadn't been there. For crying out loud, Ceejz, you were the one who clued the doctors and probably saved her spoiled little life."

"Lissa is *not* spoiled!" Spinning, C.J. took two stomped steps, slammed the water bottle on the kitchen counter. "She is a brilliant, funny, loving child. Don't you dare say anything unkind about her. You don't even know her, you have no idea what it's like to...to..." The angry outburst fizzled with her roommate's knowing smile.

"I rest my case," Bobbi said softly. "You adore that kid."

C.J. couldn't deny it.

"And you adore her father, too."

"Yes."

"So you admit that you love them both." Folding her arms, Bobbi fixed her with a slitty-eyed stare. "The question is, how much do you love them?"

Tears pricked her eyes. "Enough to let them go."

Draped across the back of the lounge chair, Rags gazed listlessly out the front window, a boneless, hairy, brown-and-white lump of pure canine misery. The animal blinked, stared at the vacant curb in front of the house, taking notice only of small white cars bearing a faint resemblance to the one belonging to the beloved mistress he hadn't seen in more than a week. The heartbroken animal would raise his head long enough to study similar vehicles as they passed, then return his chin to his paws with a pained sigh.

Rags hadn't eaten in two days.

Richard approached bearing gifts. "Here, boy, look what I found lurking in the fridge." He dangled a juicy hunk of roasted chicken in front of Rags's dejected little nose. The dog gave the item a bland look before refocusing his plaintive gaze out the window. "Well, how about a doggy treat?" Richard wrapped the chicken in a napkin, retrieved a dog biscuit from his pocket. "Look, the same kind C.J. always carries."

At the sound of her name, Rags reared his head hopefully, only to lower it with a reproachful grimace when Richard's shoulders slumped. "She's not here, boy. I'm sorry."

Rags whined.

"I know you miss her." He stroked the animal's furred

head. "But you have to eat. C.J. would be very upset if she knew you weren't taking care of yourself." The dog issued no response, although Richard was chagrined to realize that he'd actually been waiting for one. Sometimes he had to remind himself that despite undeniable intelligence, Rags was not a person in a dog suit. He was just an animal, a small, furred creature with eyes full of love and a stoic little dog heart that couldn't comprehend the pain of abandonment and loss.

Richard could relate, although grown men were not allowed to display their grief as openly as were animals and small children. It was some kind of societal rule, he supposed. But it was a damned stupid rule.

Strength was an illusion he maintained for Lissa's sake. Inside, Richard wept. He wept out of emptiness, and despair, and a loneliness so deep that even tears couldn't reach it.

Love was a frightening emotion. It exposed weakness, vulnerability. It shook the body with power and passion, illuminating strength of spirit, spotlighting shortcomings.

Richard had thought he'd been in love before, but he'd never experienced anything like this agony of the soul. He felt as if he'd been torn in two, as if he'd lost an intrinsic part of himself. He felt lost, alone. Incomplete.

Apparently Rags did, too.

Only Lissa had accepted C.J.'s departure without visible concern. While in the hospital she'd asked why C.J. hadn't come to see her, and had seemed bewildered by Richard's explanation that C.J. had feared upsetting her. The child had never asked again, nor had she responded to Richard's gentle probing as to her motive for having consumed the chocolate that had made her so deathly ill in the first place. Each of his questions had been met with a silent shrug.

So Richard had stopped asking; Lissa had stopped talking; and Rags had stopped eating.

All in all, it had not been a good week.

Giving up his quest to tempt the appetite of his daughter's unhappy pet, Richard returned the rejected chicken to the kitchen, and heard familiar puppet "voices" emanating from Lissa's room. Since the child had barely spoken since her release from the hospital days earlier, Richard considered her return to normal play as evidence of at least some emotional healing.

Pleased, he entered the hallway planning to join the child's game rather than eavesdrop upon it. But as he reached for the knob of her closed door, his ears perked and his hand wavered.

"You are such a bad girl," Lissa was saying in her deep, wizard-puppet voice. "You gave Lissa the cookie, so it's all your fault she got sick."

"I didn't mean to," came the falsetto reply.

"You are a bad girl, Suzie. C.J. doesn't like you anymore."

The deep-voice pronouncement was followed by a high-pitched shriek of dismay. "But C.J. always smiles at me in class and tells me how good I dance. I'm her very best favorite!"

A deep reply. "Uh-uh. Lissa is her favorite, and you made her sick, so C.J. never wants to see you again."

A high-pitched wail. "Oh, no!"

"Lissa is real special to C.J.," wizard-Lissa intoned. "She's her very bestest friend in the whole wide world, so you just hafta go away now 'cause you're trying to make C.J. like you better than Lissa, and that's not very nice.''

The conversation continued, but Richard wasn't listening. He stumbled back a step, sagged against the wall unable to believe what he'd already heard, yet unable to deny it. When C.J. had suggested that Lissa might have deliberately made herself ill, he'd been flabbergasted, indignant and outraged all at once. After all, a father knew his own child.

Richard did know his child, but it was C.J. who truly understood her. She'd recognized symptoms of jealousy that Richard had so blithely ignored. She'd tried to tell him, tried to explain, but he'd pushed her away, dismissed her concerns as being meritless, even foolhardy. In point of fact, Richard hadn't wanted to believe. The truth had been too frightening.

Yes, C.J. had been right. But she'd also been wrong. It wasn't Richard's time and attention Lissa had so jealously guarded. It was C.J.'s.

Dressed in formal business attire as was his habit, Thompson McCade stood stiffly on the patio, perspiring in the oppressive summer heat. He puffed his pipe, gazed across the manicured back lawn as if he hadn't heard his son-in-law's gruff question.

Richard repeated it. "You knew, didn't you?"

It took a few more seconds before McCade took a final puff, then removed the pipe, held it in his hand and gazed into the smoldering bowl. "I was aware of Lissa's admiration for Ms. Moray, yes."

"You knew more than that." Rising from the patio chair, Richard set his jaw and folded his arms. "You knew that Lissa craved C.J.'s undivided attention to the point of blind jealousy toward anyone she perceived as a threat to that attention, including me.''

McCade continued to study the smoke wafting from his pipe. ''Yes.''

Frustrated and furious, Richard clamped his jaw twice before he trusted his voice. ''Why didn't you tell me?''

''I shouldn't have had to.'' He angled an accusing glance. ''You would have seen it yourself if you hadn't been too besotted with that woman to recognize the needs of your own child.''

A dull throb in his upper arms served as a reminder that he was digging his fingers into his own flesh. Richard unfolded his arms, flexed his stiff hands. Anger drained slowly, cautiously, replaced by a resigned sense of sadness. McCade was right. Richard should have known. ''I knew Lissa was jealous of the time C.J. and I spent together. I assumed—'' He fell silent, shaking his head.

McCade completed the thought. ''You assumed that it was your attention Lissa was reticent to share.''

''Yes.''

''A logical conclusion. Erroneous, of course, but logical.'' Despite the pomposity of the words, McCade's voice displayed a compassion peculiar for a man who disdained empathy as weakness. ''I, too, was taken aback when she confided in me.''

Richard wasn't surprised by that. Lissa had always shared secrets with her adoring grandfather. A thought struck him. ''If Lissa was so fond of C.J., why was she upset to learn I wanted to marry her?''

McCade regarded him for a moment, then his guilty gaze skittered away. ''Perhaps Lissa feared that marriage

would prove that C.J. cared more for you than for her."
He issued a strained cough, cleared his throat without
meeting Richard's suspicious stare. "Perhaps she feared
losing C.J.'s friendship and, ah, was under the impression
that once you married her, you'd demand all of her attention."

Richard felt ill. There was no doubt in his mind that
his father-in-law had encouraged the child's fears, perhaps even put them into her head in the first place.
"Why?" he whispered. "Why would you put thoughts
like that into your own grandchild's head?"

For a moment, McCade gave no indication that he'd
heard. He stood there, hair gleaming like gunmetal in
sunlight, gazing into space as if silently speculating the-
ories on the origin of the universe. Finally his chest ex-
panded with a deep intake of air, and he turned to meet
Richard's gaze with one of profound sadness. "I felt that
the child's affection for Ms. Moray was an expression of
disloyalty to her mother," he said quietly. "As was
yours."

Richard swayed a moment, then sat heavily in a nearby
chair. The reply was not unexpected, but that didn't
lessen its impact. Oddly enough, Richard was saddened
by his father-in-law's behavior, but he wasn't angered by
it. "I understand how you must have felt," he said finally, and was surprised that he really did. "But you
can't bring Melinda back by isolating her child, and not
allowing her to love anyone else. That's unfair."

"Yes," McCade murmured. "I see that now."

Something in the man's voice caught Richard's attention. For the first time in all the years he'd known

Thompson McCade, there was contrition in his eyes. And regret.

Before Richard could speculate on what that meant for the future of their family, the back door flew open.

Lissa dashed out, eyes huge. She gulped a breath. "Rags is sick," she blurted as tears slid down her pale cheeks. "I don't want him to die, Daddy. Please don't let him die."

Toweling her wet hair and wearing nothing but a terry-cloth robe, C.J. hurried to the front door, paused at the peephole and nearly fell over. Her mouth went dry. Her feet turned to lead. If not for the insistent buzz of the doorbell, she'd have sworn she was hallucinating.

A dull ache in her chest reminded her to breathe. She sucked in air, draped the towel around her neck and willed her trembling hand to the knob. It seemed to turn on its own. The breath she'd just taken backed up in her throat. There stood Lissa, holding Rags in her arms, and Richard, who carried a large cardboard box from which a wheeled segment of a familiar skateboard was protruding.

Before anyone could speak, Rags emitted a thrilled woof, leapt from Lissa's grasp to circle C.J.'s feet, barking happily until she scooped up the wriggling animal, hugging him fiercely as he frantically licked her face.

"I've missed you so much," she whispered, as much to Lissa and Richard as to the ecstatic pooch. She moistened her lips, spoke carefully. "Thank you for bringing him to visit. It was very kind of you."

"It's not exactly a visit," Richard said quietly. "Lissa has something to tell you."

Lissa's eyes were enormous, her face pale as bleached cotton. "Rags is sick," she announced in a voice that quivered only a little. "Because he wants to live with you."

Stunned, C.J. looked to Richard for confirmation, received it with his stoic nod.

"Lissa loves Rags very much," he said. "She wants what's best for him."

The child's heartbroken expression went through C.J. like a blade. Bewildered, she stepped back, finally recalled her manners. "Please, come in."

After a moment's hesitation, Lissa did so, followed by her father, who was watching C.J. the way a starving man eyes a meal he cannot have. His gaze devoured her, desperate yet dejected, a poignant reflection of her own yearning heart. He took a ragged breath, nodded at the box he held. "Where should I put this?"

"Hmm? Oh. Anywhere is fine."

As Richard set the box beside the front door, C.J. lowered the squirming pooch to the floor, where he promptly dashed into the kitchen, only to reappear a moment later with an impatient bark.

Lissa instantly lit up. "Ragsy wants to eat!" The child spun around, her eyes glowing with relief. "Can I feed him, C.J., please, can I? He's gotta be real hungry by now."

It was all C.J. could do to keep from snatching the precious little girl up and hugging her until she squeaked. Instead she simply nodded, watched greedily as Lissa scampered to the box to retrieve Rags's food dish and a bag of kibble. Rags ran circles around the child, followed her into the kitchen licking his furry chops.

C.J. shivered as Richard's gaze caressed her like a touch. She nodded toward the bright-eyed animal impatiently dancing at Lissa's feet as she prepared his supper. "Rags doesn't look particularly sick to me."

"A remarkable recovery," Richard agreed. He cleared his throat, clasped his hands behind his back as if fearing what they might do without restraint. "The vet couldn't find anything wrong, either, other than obvious signs of depression."

With some effort C.J. pulled her gaze from the man who had haunted her thoughts and dreams, to focus on the crafty creature chowing down with great gusto. "Depression, my old aunt's bunions. I warned you about that sly doggy devil. He was putting on a performance, manipulating you into giving him what he wanted."

"I know that. So does Lissa."

"Then why on earth did you give in?"

"Because it was clear that Rags wants to be with you."

C.J. chewed her lip, studied the gaunt stress lines bracketing Richard's mouth. She remembered the taste of that mouth, the sweetness, the warmth. The passion. She wanted it again, so desperately her heart pounded against her ribs as if seeking escape, and her belly throbbed with a longing so sharp, so acute that she feared she wouldn't be able to bear another minute without throwing her arms around him, tasting him one last time.

"What we want," she whispered, "and what we can have aren't necessarily the same thing."

A flicker of pain, a veil of heather fog as his gaze reluctantly slid away. Apparently Richard understood that she wasn't only referring to Rags, but all he said was "Yes."

Sudden weakness bent her ankles, turned her knees to water. She swallowed the faint hope ignited by his presence, steadied herself by leaning against a wall. In the kitchen, Lissa continued to stroke her beloved pet's head as Rags wolfed down his supper. The child's eyes were solemn, filled with comprehension of her impending loss. "I can't let her do this," C.J. said. "Rags means too much to her."

A comforting warmth penetrated her shoulder where Richard touched her. "For the first time in her life, Lissa is performing a purely unselfish act, putting another's happiness above her own. Please, don't take that away from her."

As if on cue, Lissa heaved a shaky sigh, wiped a pudgy fist across her wet cheek. She stood, started to walk away but hesitated, gazing down at the shaggy animal that was so dear to her.

C.J.'s heart cracked at the sight. Richard was right, she realized. Lissa had taken a giant step toward eventual adulthood by experiencing sincere compassion, and mastering the ability to empathize with the needs of another. There was no doubt in C.J.'s mind that Lissa loved her pet. Loved him enough to let him go.

With an audible sniff, Lissa gave Rags a final hug before joining her father, who was hovering just inside the front door. "I'm ready." Her lip quivered with each word.

Richard nodded, lovingly stroked her pigtailed head. "Don't you have something to say to C.J.?"

The child's brave expression crumpled. A fresh spurt

of tears spilled down her cheeks. "I...I ate the cookie on purpose."

"Oh, sweetie." C.J. knelt, gathered the trembling little girl in her arms. "I know, honey, I know. We all make mistakes. It's all right."

Sobbing now, Lissa wound her arms around C.J.'s neck, squeezing tightly enough to make breathing difficult. "I tried to get Suzie in trouble. I shouldn't have done it, I know I shouldn't have, and I'm really sorry, really, really sorry."

The impact of her words rocked C.J. back on her heels. It had never occurred to C.J. that Lissa had been motivated by anything beyond interrupting the planned marriage proposal. "But why? I thought Suzie was your friend."

Reluctantly Lissa stepped back, her little face contorted in pain, and made no protest when her father slid a comforting arm around her trembling shoulders. "'Cause...'cause..." She sniffed, wiped her wet eyes. "'Cause I didn't want you to like her better than me."

Somehow C.J.'s legs stiffened enough to lever her into a standing position, but her mind was a muddle. She gazed from the shattered child sobbing against her father's chest to Richard's sad face.

Their eyes held, exchanged emotions so powerful that her spine rocked with the impact. She saw the question in his eyes, and knew he would leave unless she stopped him.

And C.J. wanted to stop him. Her heart begged her to stop him. But just as her hand reached out, the terror swelled up, the memories of a martyred, angry mother and a father resigned to a lifetime of unhappiness.

Even worse was her confusion, dizzying, disjointed thoughts and fears that something profound had been revealed to her yet she was unable to grasp the implications. All she knew for certain was that she'd believed she understood Lissa, but she'd been wrong. What else had she been wrong about? Richard's love for her? Hers for him?

Questions circled in her mind like vultures. There were no answers—only fear, stark, cold terror of making the wrong choice, the wrong decision, of looking into Richard's eyes a decade from now and seeing the reflection of her own father's misery.

But now C.J. saw only heartbreak in Richard's eyes, and immeasurable loss. When he spoke, his voice was scraped raw. "I'm sorry," he whispered, reaching for the doorknob.

A moment later, they were gone. C.J. had never felt so alone.

"Behave yourself," C.J. told Rags. "You know the drill." The dog's tail swished hard enough to bounce his bony rump on the front porch. Satisfied, she took a deep breath, poised her finger over the doorbell. "Are you ready?" Rags barked. "Okay, here goes." She poked the button. A buzzer sounded inside. Footsteps echoed. The knob rattled. When the door swung open, C.J. pasted on a bright smile. "Hi. Long time, no see."

Richard's jaw dropped only a moment before his eyes glowed with cautious hope. "Two days, four hours and six minutes," he replied with a thin smile. "Approximately."

The corner of her mouth twitched. "A man with three

dozen clocks in the house shouldn't rely on approximations."

Behind him, a flurry of footsteps pounded the carpeted floor. "Ragsy, Ragsy, you came back!"

At the sound of Lissa's voice, the animal's tail wagged so fast it was all but invisible. He glanced up hopefully, issued a pleading whine. When C.J. nodded, the dog shot past Richard's feet and leapt into the laughing child's arms.

Grinning broadly now, Richard stepped back in silent invitation, which C.J. accepted. "I was hoping you'd bring him to visit once in a while."

"Oh, this isn't a visit." She nervously shagged her fingers through her short curls, glanced around the living room as if mentally measuring its arrangement. "You see, Rags isn't happy living with me, either."

If that pronouncement startled Richard, it seemed to horrify Lissa. "How come?" she squeaked.

"Well, it seems Rags is only happy when all of us are together." She tried for a casual shrug, eyed a vacant corner of the living room. "Do you think my antique floor lamp would look good there? I'd hate to part with it. It's been in my family for years." Her gaze moved to the dining-room table. She frowned, issued a reproachful cluck. "I'll hold you to your promise to move the clock parts. The kitchen table isn't large enough for five people."

Richard wobbled as if a puff of breath would knock him over. "Five?"

"It was my understanding that Lissa's grandparents dine here often. That makes five, doesn't it?" She glanced across the room, where Lissa and Rags were involved in noisy roughhousing. Their joyful expressions touched her heart. "Unless you plan to allow Rags to sit at the table. That would make six—"

She sucked in a quick breath as Richard cupped her face with his hands. "Are you saying what I think you're saying?"

Her palms rested against his chest, absorbing his radiating heat. "You made me an offer once. I'd like to accept it, if it's not too late."

Joy leapt from his eyes straight into his heart, but was instantly tempered by wariness. "Are you sure? I mean, what changed your mind?"

"Nothing. I've wanted to be your wife since the moment I laid eyes on you. I was just too cowardly to admit it." Emotion choked her voice, made her sound snively, but she couldn't help it. For the first time in her life, she was offering her love, her trust, her heart. It was the most frightening thing she'd ever done. It was also the most thrilling. "The truth is that Rags isn't the only one who can't be truly happy without you and Lissa. I can't, either. I love you, Richard. I'll admit that frightens me, but I can't make it go away. I will always love you. I—" her voice cracked with emotion "—I have no choice."

Richard's eyes widened in surprise, softened with warmth. Before he could respond, a tug on C.J.'s sleeve captured her attention. Lissa gazed up with huge, hopeful eyes. "Are you going to marry my daddy?"

"I want to, sweetie. Does that worry you?" When the child shrugged, C.J. embraced her. "I can't take your mommy's place, Lissa, and I don't want to. Your grandpa told me that you were worried about some things. That's okay. I understand. But I want you to know that whatever happens, I will always love you, and I will always be your friend.''

Lissa issued a moist smile. ''Always?''

''Always.'' C.J. hugged the child, angled a glance at Richard and responded to his stunned stare. ''Thompson dropped by for a visit. We had a nice talk. He's really not so bad once you get to know him.''

It took a moment for that to sink in. When it did, Richard's smile took C.J.'s breath away. She gazed deeply into his eyes, and saw hope, and joy, and love. She saw family. She saw commitment. She saw his promise of forever, and joyously accepted. Her love was irrevocable.

And for the first time in her life, C.J. wasn't afraid.

* * * * *

**HE CAN CHANGE A DIAPER IN THREE SECONDS FLAT
BUT CHANGING HIS MIND ABOUT MARRIAGE MIGHT
TAKE SOME DOING! HE'S ONE OF OUR**

Fabulous Fathers

July 1998

ONE MAN'S PROMISE by Diana Whitney (SR#1307)

He promised to be the best dad possible for his daughter. Yet when successful architect Richard Matthews meets C. J. Moray, he wants to make another promise—this time to a wife.

September 1998

THE COWBOY, THE BABY AND THE BRIDE-TO-BE
by Cara Colter (SR#1319)

Trouble, thought Turner MacLeod when Shayla Morrison showed up at his ranch with his baby nephew in her arms. Could he take the chance of trusting his heart with this shy beauty?

November 1998

ARE YOU MY DADDY? by Leanna Wilson (SR#1331)

She hated cowboys, but Marty Thomas was willing to do anything to help her son get his memory back—even pretend sexy cowboy Joe Rawlins was his father. Problem was, Joe thought he might like this to be a permanent position.

Available at your favorite retail outlet, only from

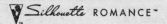

Silhouette ROMANCE™

Look us up on-line at: http://www.romance.net   SRFFJ-N

Take 2 bestselling love stories FREE

Plus get a FREE surprise gift!

Special Limited-Time Offer

Mail to Silhouette Reader Service™

3010 Walden Avenue
P.O. Box 1867
Buffalo, N.Y. 14240-1867

YES! Please send me 2 free Silhouette Romance™ novels and my free surprise gift. Then send me 6 brand-new novels every month, which I will receive months before they appear in bookstores. Bill me at the low price of $2.90 each plus 25¢ delivery and applicable sales tax, if any.* That's the complete price, and a saving of over 10% off the cover prices—quite a bargain! I understand that accepting the books and gift places me under no obligation ever to buy any books. I can always return a shipment and cancel at any time. Even if I never buy another book from Silhouette, the 2 free books and the surprise gift are mine to keep forever.

215 SEN CH7S

Name	(PLEASE PRINT)	
Address	Apt. No.	
City	State	Zip

This offer is limited to one order per household and not valid to present Silhouette Romance™ subscribers. *Terms and prices are subject to change without notice. Sales tax applicable in N.Y.

USROM-98   ©1990 Harlequin Enterprises Limited

Don't miss Silhouette's newest cross-line promotion

Five stellar authors, five evocative stories, five fabulous Silhouette series— pregnant mom on the run!

October 1998: **THE RANCHER AND THE AMNESIAC BRIDE** by top-notch talent **Joan Elliott Pickart** (Special Edition)

November 1998: **THE DADDY AND THE BABY DOCTOR** by Romance favorite **Kristin Morgan** (Romance)

December 1998: **THE SHERIFF AND THE IMPOSTOR BRIDE** by award-winning author **Elizabeth Bevarly** (Desire)

January 1999: **THE MILLIONAIRE AND THE PREGNANT PAUPER** by rising star **Christie Ridgway** (Yours Truly)

February 1999: **THE MERCENARY AND THE NEW MOM** by *USA Today* bestselling author **Merline Lovelace** (Intimate Moments)

Only in—

Silhouette Books

Available at your favorite retail outlet.

Look us up on-line at: http://www.romance.net

SSEFTB

MEN!

A good one isn't hard to
find—they're right here in
Silhouette Romance!

MAN: Vincent Pastorelli, Committed Fireman

Look out for the woman who melts Vincent's
heart in Carla Cassidy's
WILL YOU GIVE MY MOMMY A BABY? (August 1998)

MAN: Alex Trent, Wealthy Businessman

Find out how Alex convinces his best friend to
open her heart in Christine Scott's
HER BEST MAN (September 1998)

MAN: Devin Bartlett, 100% Cowboy

Meet the woman who will make Devin commit
once again in Robin Nicholas's
COWBOY DAD (October 1998)

Available at your favorite retail outlet.

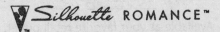
Silhouette ROMANCE™

Look us up on-line at: http://www.romance.net   SRMEN

MATERNITY LEAVE

Coming September 1998

Three delightful stories about the blessings
and surprises of "Labor" Day.

TABLOID BABY by Candace Camp

She was whisked to the hospital in the nick of time....

THE NINE-MONTH KNIGHT
by Cait London

A down-on-her-luck secretary is experiencing
odd little midnight cravings....

THE PATERNITY TEST by Sherryl Woods

The stick turned blue before her
biological clock struck twelve....

*These three special women are very pregnant...and very
single, although they won't be either for too much longer,
because baby—and Daddy—are on their way!*

Available at your favorite retail outlet.

Look us up on-line at: http://www.romance.net   PSMATLEV

twins
on the doorstep

BY STELLA BAGWELL

The Murdocks are back!
All the adorable children from the delightful
Twins on the Doorstep
miniseries are grown up and
finding loves of their own.

You met Emily in
THE RANCHER'S BLESSED EVENT
(SR #1296, 5/98)
and in August 1998 Charlie is the
lawman about to be lassoed in

THE RANGER AND THE WIDOW WOMAN
(SR#1314)

In the next few months look for Anna's and Adam's
stories—because the twins are also heading for the altar!

Only in

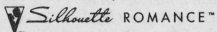

Silhouette ROMANCE™

Available at your favorite retail outlet.

Look us up on-line at: http://www.romance.net   SRTOD